ANGELS OF THE KNIGHTS

~NIKKI~

VALERIE ZAMBITO

Copyright © 2014 Valerie Zambito

All rights reserved.

ISBN-13: 978-0-9915054-1-8

Cover Art by Ravven

http://www.ravven.com

OTHER TITLES BY VALERIE ZAMBITO

ISLAND SHIFTERS - AN OATH OF THE BLOOD (BOOK 1)

ISLAND SHIFTERS - AN OATH OF THE MAGE (BOOK 2)

ISLAND SHIFTERS - AN OATH OF THE CHILDREN (BOOK 3)

ISLAND SHIFTERS – AN OATH OF THE KINGS (BOOK 4)

ANGELS OF THE KNIGHTS - FALLON (BOOK 1)

ANGELS OF THE KNIGHTS - BLANE (BOOK 2)

ANGELS OF THE KNIGHTS – NIKKI (BOOK 3)

ANGELS OF THE KNIGHTS SERIES REVIEWS

"THE STORY WAS INSANE. ONCE FALLON LEAVES EMPERICA TO HEAD BACK TO EARTH AS A KNIGHT, YOU BETTER STRAP YOURSELF IN FOR THE RIDE".

"I COULDN'T PUT IT DOWN!!!!!!!!!!!!"

"I ATE THIS BOOK UP! I THOROUGHLY ENJOYED THE AUTHOR'S STYLE OF WRITING AND THE NEW PREMISE THIS BOOK HAD."

Table of Contents

	Prologue – Battle at Baylor's Pass	1
1	Return to Compton	8
2	A Waking Nightmare	16
3	The Immortals	25
4	Devilish Plans	36
5	Magic	44
6	Doorway to Freedom	55
7	Window to Freedom	65
8	A Change of Plans	71
9	Tyras Courts	80
10	Camp Drexton	88
11	Shields	99
12	The Montero Estate	108
13	No Way Out	116
14	Answered Prayers	123
15	Impossible Dreams	130
16	Too Close to Home	137
17	Back From the Dead	149

18	Fiery Demands	159
19	Rampage	167
20	Demons and Angels	173
21	One of Our Own	183
22	Nikki's Truth	192
23	Balance	203
	Epilogue - Peace	210
	Afterword	213
	About the Author	214

"The devil's most devilish when respectable."

*- Elizabeth Barrett Browning
(Aurora Leigh)*

Prologue

Battle at Baylor's Pass

"Master, come! Master!"

An unfamiliar pull at Tyras' lips perplexed him until he recognized it for what it was—a smile. Others who witnessed it might view it as something more sinister coming from him, but the sentiment it represented could not be denied. For the first time in a very long time, genuine joy coursed though his body proving he was still capable of such emotion.

I have much to rejoice, do I not? The key is in play. Whether or not this fallen angel will be successful is yet to be determined, but the timing feels right. It is my time.

"One moment, Poati," Tyras called to the small demon waving frantically from the doorway. The creature stood four feet tall and if you could dismiss the red scaled skin, he resembled an innocent child with his shock of blonde curls and cherub face. Those who made the mistake of venturing too close, however, discovered quite the opposite to be true. Small teeth filed to sharp points were quick to dispel observers of the true nature of Poati.

Tyras turned back to the three Black Knights in the room with him. Once angels and now deadly killers. Executioners. Deliverers.

The black armor they wore from head to toe gleamed in the firelight. "If I am right, the great day of wrath will be soon upon us, my friends. You have your orders. You will deliver the final judgment on humanity. Strike hard, for in success is power like you have never known. A crown on your heads and a kingdom at your feet. Do not fail me."

"It will be as you command," the trio said in unison.

"Good." Tyras adjusted the lace peeking out from under the sleeve of his long, brown coat and strode to the door. "Very well, Poati, lead on. Show me what you will."

The demon scurried away and Tyras followed. His boots and those of his companions thudded hollowly through the warren of tunnels that led upward through the mountain of volcanic rock. Soulless, red eyes peered jealously at him from within dark shadowed niches, but none of their owners showed themselves. As was the nature of the demon to covet and seek power, several had challenged him over the years and sought to kill him. None had won. Many resented the red, scaled forms he forced them to assume while he and his

Knights retained their angelic forms. But, this was his world and his rules. When he returned to earth, the demons could do with this place as they wished.

"Come, Master!" Poati urged, stopping before an arched doorway that would lead them up three stories of stone steps to the fiery world above.

Tyras gestured the demon forward, ducked inside after him and started up. Midway, a strong wind surged through the vertical tunnel, howling noisily and flapping his coat around his body. *That's odd.* Normally, the air was quite temperate here. He paused in thought. "Poati? Has the key arrived?"

"Yes!" Poati said eagerly, rubbing his hands together.

"Why didn't you say so?" he growled angrily and pushed by the little demon. Excitement propelled his legs forward and he took the stairs two at a time. At the top, he stormed through the opening to the mountain plateau and grunted in satisfaction.

The veil! It's opening!

Hundreds of demons crowded around a boulder-sized, undulating sphere etched directly into the inky gloom that blanketed every inch of Mordeaux.

"Move!" he screamed and the fiends in his way skittered back to give him room, hissing and screeching their loathing of his command. He ignored them and stalked forward, flames licking at his boots as he moved across the scorched, cracked ground atop the volcano. He had to lean into the force of the wind as he drew closer to the veil, his white hair whipping violently around his head.

The space now clear, he stopped in front of the portal with predatory hunger, the object of his desire at long last within reach.

Earth.

Shimmering seductively before his sight. Beckoning to him with green grasses, mountains, and a darkened sky that he remembered would shine with light in the coming morn. The few glimpses of earth he managed through possessions of the Kjin did nothing to prepare him for this reality.

Now, though, a major battle raged.

Knights of Emperica wielded powerful swords of light against his earth-bound brethren. Tyras couldn't hear the fighting through the portal, but the brutality of the images told him enough. The angels were winning. All while the key stood on a rise directly in front of the portal, striking at the opening with hard, frantic strokes.

Yes, that's it! Tyras silently urged, his hands clenched into white-knuckled fists at his sides as he willed the key to move faster. *Open it up!*

Out of nowhere, a blaze of white jumped up onto the rise and the key spun around to confront the figure—a dark-haired woman. Bright sparks lit the night as the two angels exchanged blows with their swords.

Tyras stood transfixed by the battle.

The female moved with grace and determination, her arrogant features twisted with righteous cause. A quick feint put the key where she wanted him, allowing her to elbow him in the face. When he dropped to the ground, she stood over him and wrenched her Aventi over her shoulder to deliver the killing stroke.

But, the key surprised her by swinging his leg out, and the dark-haired angel stumbled back.

"Yes!" Tyras screamed out loud. "Hurry now!"

As though hearing his yell, the key staggered back to his feet and swung, drawing a long, deep gash down the center of the portal.

A high-pitched screech sprang out of the gap sending the two angels on the rise and all behind them to the ground.

He's done it! "Prepare to do battle, demons!"

Savage grunts and growls exploded all around him.

"Open the portal!" he commanded. "Black Knights! With me!"

At his order, several demons stepped forward, shoving fingers and claws into the gash to tear it apart. It didn't take long and within a few moments, the portal snapped open and the terrible noise came to a halt.

A massive swirl of sulfur-scented air blasted out of the breach, lifted the two angels on the rise and sucked them in toward the opening. The demons in front caught the key and took him to the ground, devouring him flesh and soul. Tyras reached out, seized the ankle of the female angel, and yanked her roughly down beside him. Her head hit the volcanic rock with a horrible thud.

"Go now, demons! The way to earth is clear!"

As the first of the demons made their way onto the rise, Tyras slipped out of the opening, dragging the unconscious female behind him.

A young Kjin jumped up onto the knoll, and Tyras grabbed him by the throat. "I need a weapon."

The demon started to protest until he saw the glow of Tyras' red eyes. The Kjin screamed in horror and fumbled in his pocket for a knife. After shoving the weapon in Tyras' hand, the youngster sprinted away at a dead run.

Idiot!

Tyras' glowing eyes flashed as he searched the area for a way off the mountain, and then his gaze snagged on a matter of unfinished business.

Cesar Grant.

The Kjin leader cursed and waved his arms, clearly angry at something that didn't seem to have anything to do with the actual fighting.

Tyras dropped the girl's ankle and slid silently into place behind Grant. "You failed me," he whispered. "Probably not your best move."

"Ah!" Cesar jerked around, his eyes wide with fright. "Help! Someone help me!"

Tyras smiled and locked his red eyes on Grant, pinning him in place and silencing his screams. "As I was saying, you failed me, and I made perfectly clear the penalty for failure."

Powerless to move in the grasp of Tyras' mental hold, Grant could only stand there helplessly as Tyras' newly-acquired knife sliced across his throat. His body twitched only once as his life spilled from the wound.

The grisly deed done, Tyras stepped back to let the corpse fall at his feet.

A light-haired, older Kjin ran toward him and skidded to a stop. The demon looked down at the body of his leader and then to the Black Knights stepping up behind Tyras.

"You know who I am?" Tyras asked.

The Kjin nodded warily.

"What is your name?"

"Gordon Strand."

"Where is the heart of power here, Strand?"

Gordon scratched his jaw. "Washington?"

"Pick a few allies and take me there." He pointed to the angel on the ground. "And, bring her with us."

CHAPTER 1

Return to Compton

"Good evening, I'm Tamara Elliott, reporting to you live from Harris Center in New York. Still no new leads in the violent air strikes three weeks ago on several churches and warehouses across the country that left fifty-six people dead. The Air Force helicopters used in the attacks and found abandoned days later held no clues for investigators. Was it a terrorist attack or the work of a local radical group? No official word yet from the military at Camp Drexton where the helicopters were stolen or from Tennessee Governor Tad Billingsley. Many people have vigorously criticized Billingsley and the current administration for not doing enough to explain how U.S. helicopters could have been confiscated for such a deadly homeland attack, however, the President assured the public yesterday in his state of address that a thorough investigation was ongoing. Now, on a lighter note..."

Blane turned off the television. *Three weeks.* Three weeks since they lost Nikki. Three weeks since they had been able to pick up the trail of a single Kjin. Three weeks since Father Paul in Compton disappeared. Without the Emissier, he had no way to connect with Darius and the silence from all fronts ate away at him.

Where are all the Kjin? Several hundred died in the battle at Baylor's Pass, but others should have moved in by now. His instincts screamed at him that more was at play, but what? He shook his head. He would need more Knights to get the answer to that question. The deaths of Nikki, Micah and Justus had left his Paladin team in shatters with only Fallon and her human, police officer husband, Kade Royce, to help him rebuild and continue the fight.

"Uh, oh, I know that look."

Blane turned to the doorway and the sight of his beautiful wife pushed his concerns aside. "What look is that, Juliet?" he asked and held his arms out toward her.

"The look that wants to tear apart a thousand demons. Single handedly." She walked into his embrace and circled her arms around his waist. "You're leaving, aren't you?"

He nodded. "We're going to Compton to see if we can find Father Paul. If he's not there, we'll have to travel to the closest Emissier, and he's in Chicago."

"Shit."

"I thought you weren't going to swear anymore?"

"What can I say? I'm a work in progress." A cute pout turned her lips down. "So, the honeymoon is over?"

"Never over," he growled and dragged her face up to his to place a firm kiss on her mouth. "Simply postponed every now and then when duty calls."

She turned her head and placed her cheek against his chest. "I should have married a plumber."

"I'm pretty sure his hours would be worse than mine."

"Yeah, I don't think I could deal with that whole pant thing anyway."

"So, you're sticking with me?"

"Always," she whispered. "Be careful, okay?"

He kissed the top of her head. "I'll call you from Compton and let you know what I find. Give the girls a hug for me when they wake up."

"I will. Hurry home."

Reluctantly, Blane let her go and grabbed his leather jacket off the bed. If he stayed any longer, he might never leave and Fallon and Kade were waiting for him.

On his way out, he grabbed an umbrella. Another miserable item to add to his three week list—the rain. Ever since the portal to Mordeaux was opened, it had not stopped raining. Not just here in Reglan, but all across the world. Everywhere. A relentless, dreary downpour that sapped spirits and made it difficult to do just about anything outdoors.

Ducking out through the front door, he ran to the idling car. As soon as he approached Fallon jumped out of the passenger seat with a laptop clutched under her arm. "Here, sit in front. I want to look up a few things on the drive."

Blane held the umbrella for her while she got into the back and then slid in the front seat next to Kade. The strains of an old love song from his era filled the car. He recognized it as Lionel Richie's *Three Times a Lady*. "What are you listening to?" he asked Kade with a lift of his eyebrow.

The cop's face turned scarlet. "What? This? How do I know?" he scoffed. "Something Fallon must have put on."

Fallon snorted from the back seat prompting Kade to quickly turn the station.

"You're whipped," he told Kade.

"I wouldn't talk, big guy."

Blane laughed, but quickly got down to business. He had been preoccupied with his new family over the past few weeks, but now it was time to work. "Tell me what's happening."

Kade was just as quick. "Another group of Knights showed up late last night. We're at around a hundred right now, but I'm sure more will trickle in soon."

Blane wasn't so optimistic. They lost a lot of Knights in the helicopter attacks and the battle, and he had a sinking feeling that a hundred was all that was left.

"I left Seth in charge of operations while we're gone," Kade continued.

"Good." He glanced over his shoulder at Fallon. "Any word on Father Paul?"

Fallon's fingers flew over the keyboard of her laptop. "I love these things," she mumbled to herself and then to him, "Nothing. Last known sighting was the Friday after the battle, eating alone at a local diner. First report of concern came from a church secretary when Father Paul didn't show up for Sunday mass."

"Where could he be?" Blane mused aloud as the countryside sped by outside the window. "He has to know how much we need him right now."

"The police have already gone through his home, so I would suggest starting at The Church of Mary," Fallon said.

"I agree."

The rest of the five-hour trip dragged as Blane considered what the next move of the Order should be. It still amazed him that the Elders intervened in the battle. Of course, if they hadn't, a horde of demons would have been let loose on earth, but everything he had been taught in training made it clear that Emperica could *not* get involved in the affairs of this world. Yet, they did. For the first time in history.

"We're here," Kade announced.

The church Blane visited with Juliet just weeks ago came into view and Kade pulled up in front of the building.

"Do you think anyone will be here on a Monday?" Fallon asked as they got out of the car.

Blane shrugged. "Only one way to find out." He ran through the drenching rain up the wide steps of the church and pushed inside. All was silent in the dim vestibule and a quick peek told him no one was seated in any of the pews either, so he led the way directly to Father Paul's office.

He knocked on the door. No answer. He tried the handle and, finding it unlocked, went in and scanned the room. An empty desk, half a cup of coffee, a pen laying atop a set of notes, a lamp light still on.

Kade examined the same pieces of evidence with his trained eye and came to the same conclusion as Blane. "Looks like he was interrupted by someone or something. And, he never made it back."

Fallon wiped her hand through a smudge of black fingerprint powder on a file cabinet. "Police have dusted. Wonder if they found anything."

A muffled banging noise caught Blane's attention. "Do you hear that?" he asked.

"I don't hear anything," Fallon answered

"It's coming from outside."

Fallon hurried to the window. "Oh, that must be it. There's a shed with an open swinging door outside on the grounds. Is that what you hear?"

That, and the soft whistle of the wind, the creak of the windows, a car driving by out front. Blane knew that his hearing was more acute than the others, but it all sounded so loud in his ears that it surprised him when others couldn't hear what he did.

"Let's check it out." Blane strode out of the office and went through the silent nave to a back exit. The moment he stepped outside, an acrid scent that even the rain couldn't dampen assailed his nostrils. There could be no mistaking that smell.

It was the smell of death.

He walked toward the shed, the ominous thumping door a chilling presage of what he suspected he might find. *Please let me be wrong.* A mumbled prayer sprang to his lips as he moved forward. His feet felt made of lead. His heart heavier still.

Blane stopped at the opening. Bile rose in his throat at the grisly sight of Father Paul's spread-eagled body nailed by his hands and feet to the ceiling and floor.

"Oh, no," Fallon cried, coming up next to him. "Who would do such a thing? Wait, what's that on his chest?"

"A message."

"What does it say?" Kade asked from behind.

"One of ten."

"One of...? The Emissiers?"

Blane nodded. "Fallon, start making calls. Find out the fate of the others." He turned toward Kade. "Call the police."

Kade's phone rang before he could dial, and Blane listened in on the one-side conversation.

"Royce." A pause. "What?" he snapped. "That doesn't make any sense, Seth. All right, we'll figure it out when we get back." He ended the call. "We have to get to Reglan right away."

"Why?"

"We have company at the warehouse."
"Who?"
"Says he's our new leader."

Chapter 2

A Waking Nightmare

Nikki woke and knew instantly something was wrong. The feel of a tight compress around her head brought her hand up to investigate, but halfway there a tube in her arm pulled tight. *Ouch!*

She listened to the sounds around her. To her left, a machine of some kind emitted soft, steady beeps. *A hospital?* Tentatively, she lifted her head. No, not a hospital. A bedroom. A young girl's room if the frilly curtains, pink walls and dolls lining the top of a dresser were any indication.

She had been injured, that much was certain, but how? When? The door opened pulling her away from her probing thoughts. A pretty, middle aged woman with blonde hair pulled back in a neat bun moved to her bedside and checked the fluids dripping into her arm.

"Where...am I?" Nikki asked hoarsely, dragging the words over the sandpaper lodged in her throat.

The woman jumped. "Oh, you're awake." She quickly lifted Nikki's wrist and checked her pulse. "What's your name?"

"Nikki. Nikki Falco."

"How do you feel, Nikki?"

"Tired. Where am I?" she asked again, noticing the unusual color of the woman's eyes—a shade of brown so light, they looked orange.

"You're being well taken care of, Nikki."

That's not what I asked. Perspiration trickled down Nikki's chest. "Why is it so hot in here?"

The woman pulled Nikki's sheet down to her waist to cool her off. After glancing nervously toward the door, she said softly, "It's the way Mr. Smith likes it."

"Who's Mr. Smith?"

"I was hoping you'd know."

"I don't. What happened to me?"

"You suffered a skull fracture and were placed in a medically-induced coma."

A skull fracture? Why don't I remember it? "How long have I been here?"

"Three weeks."

"Am I healed?"

Confusion wrinkled the woman's brow. "Completely. The bone is knitted back together as if it never happened."

Nikki reached out and put a hand on the woman's arm. "Please, tell me where I am."

"I...I'm not sure where we are."

Wasn't expecting that answer. "How can you not know where we are?"

The woman once again shot an uneasy look toward the door. "I'm not allowed to leave."

Nikki fought against a sudden stab of panic that made her want to rip the IV out of her arm and run. "What do you mean?"

"I...I am a physician and I was kidnapped from Knoxville three weeks ago to care for you." She sat on the bed and started removing the IV. "I know we're in some kind of large old Victorian style mansion that overlooks a river. I'm thinking we're close to D.C."

Nikki shook her head. This wasn't making any sense. She didn't know anyone in D.C. And, certainly not a Mr. Smith.

"Do you have any idea who would want to...keep you like this?" the doctor asked. "And, kidnap someone to care for you? The mob, maybe?"

Nikki flinched as the needle came out. "No, nothing like that."

The doctor vaulted to her feet. "Then what? I'm grasping at straws! I've got to get out of here and back to my family!"

Nikki turned away from the desperation in the woman's eyes. *I have no clue. Think! I remember being at the warehouse and greeting a group of new Knights. We were gathering for something. There was a mountain top. Blane pacing. A speech about our need to fight...*

"Now, that you're better," the doctor continued on the verge of tears, "they don't need me anymore. I'm terrified they're going to kill me."

Nikki sat up and ripped the sheets the rest of the way off. "I'll protect you. Just stay calm until I figure this out. Can you describe the people in the house?"

The doctor gave her a hard look revealing her doubts about Nikki's protective abilities. "Several men come and go. A few others guard the exits at all times, but the only people actually living in the house are Mr. Smith, a housekeeper and...a child."

"A child?"

"A little boy around five or six." She shuddered. "It's strange. His skin is painted or dyed red and his teeth are sharpened to points. A bizarre Halloween costume possibly. Or some tribal significance. I'm not sure."

Nikki drew in a sharp breath as she abruptly recalled similar red skin. *No, doctor, not a costume at all. A demon.*

∽

Blane pushed open the door to the warehouse harder than he intended and it slammed open causing all eyes to swing his way. After learning that every single Emissier of Emperica had been murdered and then dealing with five hours of speculation regarding this new *leader*, he was in no mood for games.

He stalked forward and the Knights in his path stumbled back away from him revealing three newcomers standing before the gathering. One, a tall man with dark-blonde hair and a few days worth of stubble on his chin, wore a sleeveless vest showing off the numerous tattoos that covered his arms. Another appeared to be in his late forties but with a full head of gray hair. Of medium height, he had a pugilistic build, all wiry corded muscle, and carried what looked like a silver, coiled whip on his belt. The third was a child of no more than eleven or twelve and completely bald. A short, silver bow dangled over one shoulder. If he had any arrows, Blane didn't see them.

"What's going on here?" he demanded. As he neared the trio, recognition set in. "August? August Rand?"

The blonde-haired man stepped forward with an outstretched hand. "Blane. Good to see you again."

Blane grunted and took it, surprised to see one of Darius' top Knight trainers. "First a visit from Darius and now you?"

"I'm taking over."

"I appreciate the offer, but we got it here."

"It wasn't an offer."

Blane's gaze narrowed at the tattooed Knight and the unusual blade he wore at his hip. Like the other weapons, it, too, was silver and also much shorter than the Aventis Blane and his Knights utilized. It looked more like a dagger than a sword. He recalled Darius' assurance that the next Knights sent to earth would be better prepared to put the Kjin faction down once and for all. "Is that our new defense against the demons?" he asked, pointing with his chin toward the dagger. "Looks kind of puny."

Some of the Knights chuckled softly.

In a blur of movement, August circled behind Blane and hovered the dagger across his throat. "Unlike your Aventi, this puny dagger can kill demon *and* shade with a single touch." August's breath was hot on his neck. "I like my kills up close and personal."

All fell silent in the room, the tension thick.

Then, Blane threw his head back and laughed. He could almost hear the collective release of breath from the Knights.

August patted him on the back and sheathed his weapon. "It's good to see you, old friend."

"You, too. If someone has to take over the leadership," Blane told him honestly, "I'm glad it's you. All right, show us what you can do."

August walked back and stood next to his two comrades. At a nod from him, their human forms melted away and they shifted into luminescent, angelic wraiths.

A communal gasp reverberated throughout the room.

Blane looked on in awe as three pairs of majestic wings snapped open and lifted behind each of the angels. White, beautiful layers of pure perfection that caused Blane's shoulder blades to twinge in envy.

"What happened?" Kade asked out loud. "Where did they go?" His human eyes couldn't see what Blane and the rest of the Knights saw.

"As you can see, we have the ability to alter into wraith form," August said, ignoring Kade's question. "Invisibility, flight and our new weapons will give us a major advantage over the demons. The Kjin will never know we're coming until it's too late." He turned toward the angels with him and stopped before the gray-haired man. "This is Vincent. He wields a silver lasso with a whip attached that can kill a demon with a single bite." He turned to the boy. "And, this is Joseph, our archer. His projectiles can track and hit a Kjin at a thousand yards." The bald, blue-eyed boy smiled and bowed his head.

The Knights murmured in approval, clearly impressed.

"We're not sure if they will work as efficiently on the Black Knights, so—"

"Black Knights? What are you talking about?"

August reverted to his human form, color and contour filtering back into his body. "Is there somewhere we can talk in private?"

"Wait, answer something for me. I was working with a Knight. Her name was Nikki. Do...do you know if she made it back to Emperica?"

A pained expression crossed August's features. "I do know her, but I'm not sure if she made it back or not. After the Elders' impromptu visit here to earth, I had no time for anything other than planning our return."

The news crushed Blane and he sighed heavily. "It would be nice to know for sure."

"Sorry, mate."

Blane started toward the back of the warehouse. "Come on. We can talk back here." He guided August to his small office and shut the door to give them privacy.

"There's more," August said right away.

Blane leaned back against his desk with his arms crossed. "Tell me."

"We're Immortals."

Blane grimaced. "Immortals? But, that means you'll be earthbound forever. You'll never return to Emperica." The idea of never again experiencing the heavenly utopia he knew waited for him was unbearable to think about. Every action, every breath, every thought, took him one step closer to home.

"It's a sacrifice we made willingly."

"But, why? We made a huge dent in the Kjin. The Order is now organized into an elite force. With a few more Knights from Darius, we can do this, August!"

August took out a rolled newspaper from his back pocket and shoved it in Blane's hand. "Read and tell me what it means."

Blane scanned the headlines on the front page. None of the stories seemed out of the ordinary, albeit a little more depressing than usual. Six mass murders across the country, four school shootings, a government shutdown, floodings, an earthquake, an ecoli breakout in six states. Which article do you want me to read?"

"Not one, all. Look at the dates. Every one of these events occurred within the past three weeks, Blane."

"Since...the battle," he thought out loud.

"Yes."

"And...?"

"It's not just the demons we're here to fight. It's Tyras. The devil is alive and active in the world. The evil that has sprung up, this string of disorder that plagues our society, are all the result of Tyras' perverse hand."

"Wait. Are you saying that his reach has grown? That he now has the ability to directly affect events from Mordeaux?"

"No. I'm telling you that he's *here*, Blane. Tyras walks the earth again."

CHAPTER 3

The Immortals

August picked up a framed photograph off the desk. It was a picture of Blane, Fallon and Nikki in happier times. Laughing. Nikki with two fingers sticking up behind Blane's head.

He smiled even as a sharp pull in his chest gripped him at seeing Nikki's face again. None of the others knew that he and Nikki had known each other and, in fact, died together. It had been many years ago, well over thirty, but he remembered that terrible night like it was yesterday. How could he ever forget killing the girl he loved?

When they reunited in Emperica, their relationship had none of the intensity it did when they were alive. It wasn't meant to. But, now back here on earth and staring into vibrant brown eyes that even a photo couldn't mute, all of the old feelings rushed through him like a tidal wave.

"So, what's the plan?"

August straightened at Blane's question and returned the photograph to the desk. "I need you to assemble a field unit of the best you have and go after Tyras' Black Knights."

"Who are these Black Knights?"

His jaw clenched in anger. "Angels at one time. Three members of the original twelve that sided with Tyras in the Holy War. They've returned with him and their purpose appears to be wrecking havoc while the devil plots in the shadows. War, strife, murder. Whatever it takes to cause death and destruction. Like Tyras, these fallen angels loathe humans and take immense pleasure in their suffering. They have to be stopped at all costs."

"How do we track them?"

"Grunt work. Follow the leads. Talk to people. Interrogate Kjin. But, be extremely vigilant. Your Kur won't detect them, but *they* can track you. These Black Knights have the ability to sense angels. All of which means we should get out of here as soon as possible. We're sitting ducks with this many Knights in one place."

"What will you be doing?"

"I'm leaving tonight for Roanoke to meet with Sam Barnes and make sure we get the President underground. It will probably take a few days at the least."

"Sam Barnes?"

"The Deputy Director of the Secret Service. He's a Knight."

"That's new news," Blane said in shock. "All right. I'll get a research team working right away to see if they can pinpoint where these Knights are. As soon as they find something solid, I'll take Fallon and Kade out with me."

August lifted his eyebrows. "I hope you're not referring to the human you walked in with. You'll have to move fast for this, Blane, and he won't be able to keep up."

"But, he—"

"No. You'll take one of the Immortals. Leave the human behind. That's an order."

He finally nodded. "Understood. I'll take Vin—"

A loud crash sounded outside of the warehouse followed by screams of pain.

August stormed out of the office and pushed through the group of Knights trying to get outside. Blane shouted to clear a path and it worked.

Once out the door, August ran out onto the wide sidewalk in front of the warehouse and pulled up short. An enormous, black-armored figure at least six and a half feet tall stood in the middle of the street with a sword in one hand and a shield in the other.

The heavy rain kept most people in the busy commercial district indoors, but those that were out scattered in all directions as they raced to escape the madman. The wreckage of an overturned van shot smoke and sparks into the air, its occupants struggling to crawl free.

"A Black Knight, I presume?" Blane asked beside him.

"Yes."

"I got this," one of Blane's Knights yelled out and charged at the figure, his Aventi flaring to life in his hands.

The black demon turned his armored head toward the oncoming angel and stood ready. Waiting.

"Call him back!" August demanded, but he knew it was going to be too late even as Blane did as he asked. "And, have others clear the area of witnesses. Now!"

August turned back, trusting Blane to follow his orders. He watched the running angel make an impressive leap into the air and swing his Aventi with enough strength to take the demon's head from his shoulders—armor and all—but, it didn't even make a dent. The sword of light bounced harmlessly off the black creature in a spray of white sparks sending the angel sprawling to the ground. The Black Knight was on him in a heartbeat and brought his shield slamming down on the angel's head with sickening force.

Two more angels—who either didn't hear Blane's order or didn't care after seeing one of their own fall—ran out to engage the Black Knight and lost their lives for it.

August stood out front with his palms up. "Stand down, Knights! You can't beat this demon!" What they needed was to test one of the Immortal weapons. One that could strike at a distance. "Vincent! Joseph!"

The gray-haired Immortal pushed to the front. "Right here. Stay back and let me put this whip to good use."

Vincent stalked out onto the street and stopped, settling his feet into a wide stance as he prepared his weapon. He gripped the handle in one hand and twisted a few feet of rope around his wrist letting the rest uncoil at his feet. Lifting his arm overhead, he flicked the whip back and forth a few times, testing its reach. Then, with a groan of effort, snapped it out toward the Black Knight.

The demon, perhaps sensing something different about the silver weapon, dove out of the way.

Come on, Vincent. You can do it, August urged silently.

Vincent advanced and hurled his weapon again at the fallen demon. The Black Knight rolled on his back and thrust his shield out in front of him just in time to catch the tip of the whip on the edge. Vincent tried several more times to get past the shield, but the demon deflected every strike and was now back on his feet.

"I'm sending in a diversion!" Blane yelled out and one of the female Knights peeled away from the group at his gesture.

August's shoulders twitched, at odds with that command, but he didn't say anything.

The angel made a wide circuit around the duo putting as much distance as possible between her and Vincent to keep the demon off balance. The Black Knight kept his shield up toward Vincent in one hand and his sword in the other pointed at the angel. Then, in a surprise move, the demon flipped the sword into the air, caught the grip and drove the weapon down into the ground in front of him.

An unearthly, high-pitched screech streamed out of the puncture site sending August reeling back. He covered his ears with his hands in an effort to stop the needles of pain stabbing at his brain.

Black, crackling electricity ran up and over the demon's sword, twisting sinuously over blade and hilt. *He's getting help from Mordeaux!* The Knight cackled with laughter as he filled his sword with black death.

The screeching abruptly stopped.

The demon pulled his sword from the ground and whipped it out toward the female angel. An inky rope of lightning streaked toward her and drilled a hole right through the middle of her chest. The angel stopped and looked down in a brief moment of surprise before toppling to the ground. Dead.

Vincent growled, threw down his lasso and ran at the demon apparently deciding brute force was all that was left to him. He crossed the distance before the demon had a chance to react and jumped in the air, his back arched and his hands entwined over his head. A two-fisted blow slammed down onto the demon's helmet, leaving a bowl-sized dent in the top. The Black Knight roared and swung his shield at Vincent. The Immortal just managed to avoid being hit and the two combatants traded brutal blows one after the other.

Over the grunts of the fighting pair, August watched Joseph walk evenly into the center of the street. The boy dropped to one knee and removed the bow from his shoulder. Both bow and boy burst into a halo of illumination as he brought the Black Knight into his sights.

"Vincent! Arrow!" August screamed in warning.

The Immortal heard and understood, springing clear of the demon.

Joseph calmly pulled the bowstring to his cheek. No arrow was notched, but as soon as the wire thrummed in release, a rod of white light whizzed forth and slammed into the Black Knight. Holy light engulfed the demon's entire body from within, pouring out of every seam of his armor. A final defiant scream echoed through his helm before he winked out of existence. A ghastly afterimage hung in the air for a split second before vanishing completely from sight.

Without a word, Joseph stood and walked back through the mob of angels into the warehouse.

Blane stepped up to August's side. "I'll take the archer with me."

⚜

"No."

"Yes."

"No."

"Yes! Kade, be reasonable!"

"What is reasonable about letting you go off alone to fight black-armored demons? You need me."

"I won't be alone," Fallon pointed out.

"No, you'll have Blane and a child," he answered sarcastically.

Standing under a single umbrella, Fallon grabbed two fistfuls of Kade's shirt and pulled him close. "Don't make me use my Aventi on you."

One eyebrow twitched. "Didn't work then, won't work now."

She could smile now looking back at when she tried to erase Kade's memory, but at the time, it nearly killed her. But, there was no way she could take him with her this time. August was right. They had to move fast to destroy this threat, especially after just witnessing how formidable they were. She decided to appeal to his chivalrous nature. "Blane needs you to watch out for Juliet and the girls."

"Juliet is going to be just as pissed as I am."

Blane picked just that moment to slam out of the warehouse, mumbling furiously under his breath.

"See?" Kade confirmed with a smirk.

"You heard what August said, Kade."

"August Rand cares nothing for you. I do. That should count for something."

It does, babe. But, this time, I have to put the humans I protect before you. "You have to stay behind, Kade, it's already decided. Please say you understand because I really don't have time to argue any longer."

His blue eyes held hers for a very long time, accessing, memorizing. He only pulled away when his phone buzzed and he looked down to read the text. "Looks like you'll get your wish. I have to go. When do you leave?"

"Now. We've already got a lead on a train accident in Berlin. Eye witness reports mention a figure in black on the rampage."

With one hand holding the umbrella, he used the other to snake around her waist and crush her against him with rough need. His lips found hers and he kissed her mouth as if he were starving and she was his last meal. She returned his passion, putting all her love into the kiss. Letting him know that she didn't want to be parted from him any more than he did.

Finally, he forced himself away. "Go," he said, leaning in to place one last kiss on her forehead. "But, be careful."

He handed her the umbrella and ducked into the rain. Fallon watched him get into his car, the gloom of the day adding to her dismal mood. When he was gone, she ran over to Blane's minivan, folded up her umbrella and slipped inside the passenger seat. "Ready?"

He nodded. "Just waiting for Joseph. It's about an hour drive to Berlin, so we're going to have to break a few traffic laws to get there."

"Nothing new." She glanced at him. "Everything all right with Juliet?"

"Fine," he said brusquely, his tone implying that it was anything but. Fallon knew that Blane's wife could be just as overbearing as Kade when it came to their work. It seemed odd to her now that Kade didn't press harder to go with her, but it was just as well. If he had, she might have broken down and confessed.

And, there was no way her husband would *ever* have let her go if he knew what she found out just that morning.

CHAPTER 4

Devilish Plans

"Ah, the patient is awake."

The doctor let out a frightened yelp and Nikki twisted her head to the door.

Every childhood nightmare could not prepare her for the man before her. White, shoulder-length hair parted on the side and swooped over his forehead. A face chiseled from a block of stone with a wide, strong jaw. He was tall, broad and surprisingly handsome until one's gaze landed on the red eyes glowing with malice. Eyes that held not a single trace of humanity.

Awakened memories clawed through Nikki's mind and she shook her head in denial. "No..." She fell back through darkness to the battle at Baylor's Pass. The screams, the violence, the terror all came rushing back to her. "No..." Justus trying to open the portal. The piercing scream that sent her to her knees in agony. The howling wind that lifted her and sucked her through the veil. *The veil?* "No..." The smell of sulfur. The insufferable heat. A hard, grip on her ankle. Then, blackness. Her falling body slammed to a halt, shattering all denials in the face of the hard truth.

She was face to face with the devil.

"What is her name, Dr. Morris?"

"It's...it's Nikki."

The red eyes widened in surprise. "What a strange coincidence."

Nikki's mind whirled as she readied herself to fight when all she wanted to do was scream. Tyras came closer and stood at the foot of her bed. His red stare paralyzed her with fear, sucking the scream from her mouth in a breathless whisper. She couldn't speak or move.

"Dr. Morris, you may leave us."

The woman hesitated a moment before finally turning and leaving the room as directed.

"How are you feeling, Nicola?"

Whatever hold Tyras had on her loosened and her breath gushed from her lungs. Her eyes immediately searched the room for her Aventi.

The devil gave her an oily smile. "You will find no weapon here, Nicola."

"It's Nikki," she spit at him.

"Bah," he said, waving a thick hand in the air. "Nikki is far too crass. From now on, you shall be Nicola."

"How...did you get out?"

Tyras crossed his arms at his chest. "Despite all your considerable attempts to derail the fallen Knight, he was able to open the portal to Mordeaux."

Despair coursed through her body. Tyras was *free!* Everything the angels fought to preserve was now at an end. They had failed. Not just the Creator but all of mankind. Tears pooled in her eyes, but she batted them back, refusing to cry in front of Tyras. "What happened to the other Knights?"

"Dead."

A stinging burn wedged in her throat. Fallon? Blane? Gone? Her heart broke for what Kade and Juliet must be going through. "Why am I still alive, then? What do you want with me?"

He shrugged. "You intrigue me. When I saw you fight, when I saw the determination and beauty of your face, it did something to me. Something I've not felt in a long time."

"What could the devil know about beauty?" she asked with contempt. "You seek to destroy beauty and all that is good in this world!"

"Ah, but you are very wrong, young Knight." He stepped forward to run a finger down her cheek and it felt like the sear of a fiery branding. Once again, he captured her in his piercing, hypnotic gaze and she was helpless before him. "I can very much appreciate beauty. In fact, lust fills me right this minute at the sight of you."

Inside, she screamed in disgust and tried to wriggle free of his mental grasp, but couldn't so much as twitch an eyebrow.

"But, my lovely girl, on the other point, you are absolutely correct. I do wish to destroy the world as it is today. Very much." Tyras leaned down and she felt the heat roll off him in waves so hot it felt like she should see flames dancing along his skin. He pressed his scorching lips to hers, his breath coming in excited, hungry pulls. "And, I shall do it all with you by my side."

He let her go and Nikki did scream then, at the top of her lungs.

Tyras cursed and ordered Dr. Morris back into the room. Through her hysteria, Nikki felt the pinprick of a needle in her arm.

Then, mercifully, all went dark.

⁂

When Nikki opened her eyes sometime later, she was alone. She tried to sit up and her stomach roiled in protest. Lying back down, she sifted through the thick layer of fog that coated her thoughts. It all came back to her. Tyras' arrival to her room, his leering red eyes and filthy kiss. Dr. Morris rushing in to sedate her.

With the back of her hand, she scraped harshly at her lips where she could still feel the heat of his burning mark.

She tried to puzzle everything together. Somehow, Tyras came through the portal in the chaos of the battle and brought her back out with him. What did that mean? Humans already suffered immeasurably due to the taint of the Kjin, so it was hard to imagine the effect Tyras' presence would have.

And, her friends were all gone? How had Tyras managed that?

Well, I'm not dead yet, she thought fiercely, forcing all thoughts of the others now lost to her from her mind. Determination to be free of this evil monster swung her legs over the side of the bed and pushed her to her feet.

Fighting through the dizziness, she stumbled unsteadily toward the door, knowing it would be locked, and it was. Next, she lurched to the window and ripped the curtain aside only to find a barred window. She gripped the black iron bars and pulled, but they didn't budge. She doubted she would be able to move them even at full strength, yet still she gritted her teeth and heaved, bracing her legs against the wall for leverage. *Come on!*

Finally, giving it up as useless—at least for now—she dropped her legs back to the ground and ran a hand through her long hair. *There has to be some way out of this prison!* Her gaze landed on a television in the corner of the room. She hurried over, turned it on and found a news channel.

A young reporter stood on a busy city street with a wrecked vehicle in the background. She waved a hand behind her. "I'm on the scene at Lexington Boulevard where a man stabbed four people to death just a few short hours ago. No official word yet on the identity of the perpetrator or a possible motive for this senseless act." The camera panned out to include a middle-aged woman biting nervously on her lip. "With me now is Dorothy Allen, a witness to this horrifying crime. Dorothy, can you tell us what you saw?"

Dorothy frowned at the black microphone shoved under her mouth. "Honestly, I'm not quite sure what I saw." She gave a sidelong glance at the covered bodies lying on the ground. "There was this really big man with a sword standing in the street. The victims attacked him with...glowing weapons and he killed them."

"Glowing weapons?" the reporter asked. "Like a taser?"

"No! Glowing! I'm still not quite—"

"Armageddon! Armageddon! The end is near!" The camera swung to the right and captured a man running along the street. He stopped to point to a group of people standing by a warehouse. "Angels! Those people are angels! They're here to fight the last battle. Run, people! Hide! The end is near!"

Nikki's jaw dropped. Tyras lied. The Knights were still alive! But, that wasn't what froze her in surprise. It was the tattooed man standing beside Blane and Fallon.

August Rand.

How can that be? As one of Darius' top trainers, August never had plans to come back to earth. *Or, did he?* It wasn't as though the two of them had any real interaction in Emperica.

A sad smile pulled at her lips as she looked at his face. Fallon once asked her if she had ever been in love and she answered no, but seeing August again brought such a tender ache to her heart that she wondered if that had been true. The sight of him transported her back in time to a forbidden budding romance. To warm kisses on her throat and lips. To stolen moments at a nearby park against her parents' wishes.

He wore the same sleeveless vest he had been wearing when she last saw him over thirty years ago. On screen, he turned toward the man screaming about Armageddon, green eyes narrowed dangerously. *Well, whatever brought him here is none of my concern. I have to get back to the Knights! Right now!* Her head screamed at her that this new urgency had nothing to do with reuniting with August Rand, but her thudding heart proved her head a liar.

After a soft knock on the door, Dr. Morris poked her head inside. "Nikki?"

"I'm right here."

The doctor shook her head and came inside the room. "You shouldn't be up and about yet. Now, get back in bed."

Nikki gasped. "Dr. Morris, what happened to you?" The woman had aged in the few hours since she last saw her. New crinkles lined her eyes and brow. Her skin now had a slightly yellow pallor.

Dr. Morris' hand flew to her neck. "I...I don't know. The people, the food, the water. Everything seems to rot in this house. I need to get out of here, Nikki! I have three children at home that need me." The doctor covered her face with her hands and began to sob.

Nikki put her hands on the woman's shoulders. "Dr. Morris, I will help you, but you have to promise me something." She lifted the woman's chin to make sure she heard. "You have to promise me that you won't give me any more narcotics. I can't get us out of here if you do that."

The doctor's tear-filled eyes steadied on her. "I like your spirit, Nikki, I really do, but these people aren't normal! I've heard and seen strange things. Things that don't make any sense to me."

"I know. Look, I'm going to need a weapon. Can you find something that would work? A knife, a fork? Heck, I'll settle for a spoon at this point."

"Yeah, I can try."

"How about a key? You must have one to get in here."

"No, there's a guard outside that lets me in."

"All right. Go and bring me back something. Anything. I'm going to fight our way out of here, Dr. Morris."

The doctor wiped her eyes. "I guess I don't really have much to lose at this point."

Nikki ushered the woman out and leaned her forehead against the closed door. Whatever else happened, she vowed to see Dr. Morris safely back to her children. Nikki took a few deep breaths and turned back to the room—straight into a rock hard chest.

"Ah! What...?"

Tyras held up a spoon. "Looking for this?"

She sprang back from him, wary, every muscle tensed. "How did you get in here?"

Tyras lunged forward and backhanded her. "There is no way out, Nicola! None. You will remain here at my sufferance until I am done with you. And, how long that is, my dear, depends on you. It could be next week, a year from now or this very day! Do you understand?"

She lifted a fist to her bloodied mouth.

"Do not test me, Nicola. I want you by my side."

"For what?" she yelled.

He laughed, a cold and bitter sound. "When the Creator gave life to humans, he expected all of his angels to bow to them and love them as much as he did. But, I could not love such a flawed, despicable specimen. It was foolish then and still is. The Knights blame the Kjin for all the evil on earth, but it's not the Kjin! It's the nature of these little rodents called humans!"

"That's a lie."

"It is the truth."

"And, you want me—"

"For my wife!" he roared. "No human would ever do for me. It must be you! I want you, Nicola."

Wife?

"I will rebuild what the Creator destroyed when he placed the humans above the angels."

"You plan to kill the humans here on earth?"

"Not all," he answered. "Those with the requisite expertise and talents necessary to keep me alive and happy will be spared as slaves."

I've got to stop him!

"You will do all that I say, Nicola, or you will die. Your fate is in your own hands."

Chapter 5

Magic

Black smoke billowed out from the derailed train cars scattered along the tracks like discarded, broken toys. The choking smell of burning fuel hung heavy in the air. Even now, close to an hour after the accident, people still walked around dazed and bleeding. The busy commuter trains would have been filled to capacity at the time of the derailment.

As soon as Blane pulled the car over to the side of the road, Fallon hurried out into the rain toward an overpass that would allow her a good view of the scene below.

Absently, she rubbed her belly. Although only a few weeks along, she could already feel the changes in her body—subtle, but there. *Will I ever meet you, little one?* Like the rest of them, this miracle of life inside her was now in jeopardy because the devil walked the earth.

What hope was there really? The Knights didn't have the ability to deal with this primordial threat. They were mere pawns in a crusade between two ancient adversaries, and all the signs were there that the final battle between good and evil was near. Did that mean the Creator would once again descend from the heavens to fight Tyras? Would the world be broken and ultimately remade by the victor? For that matter, would humanity still be standing at the end? One thing *was* certain. Many Knights would die before any of the questions were answered.

Where are you Tyras? Why haven't you shown your hideous face?

"When we find the Black Knight, leave him to me," Joseph said softly, coming to stand next to her.

She turned to look at him and the silver bow he carried in his hands. So innocent, yet so lethal. She hated to think of him that way, but he would be a fearsome resource in this war and one she hoped would give her child a chance at life. She vaguely wondered how he died and how he came to be chosen as an Immortal, but decided now was not the time to ask.

"We better get down there," Blane said, eyeing the wreck. "I wonder where the emergency personnel are. Why aren't the police getting this under control?"

"That's why," Joseph said.

Fallon followed where he pointed toward a section of trains that had the most damage. A dark figure holding a black sword and shield taunted a dozen frightened commuters, pinning them behind one of the overturned cars. Several dead policemen lay at his feet.

One woman stood and tried to make a run for it, but the Black Knight caught her and ripped something from her arms. Fallon squinted through the rain. It was a small child.

The woman screeched in misery, and while the others saw an opportunity to escape and jostled each other for the lead position out of there, she bravely pursued the demon now disappearing into one of the still upright train cars with her child.

Without thinking, Fallon vaulted over the bridge and plummeted thirty feet to the ground below. She grunted from the hard landing, but quickly found her balance and took off at a sprint, Blane right beside her.

"I'll lure the demon back outside," she shouted at him. "You and Joseph get in position to deal with him when I do."

If Blane answered, she didn't hear it, her attention focused on the woman and child. Hopping up onto the metal platform at the back of the train, she shouldered through the door with a savage growl. The woman's screams, loud in her sensitive ears, sent adrenaline surging through her limbs.

The Black Knight stood in the aisle and held the child—a girl—by an ankle, letting her dangle in the air while the mother tried to tear her free.

"Put her down!" Fallon screamed, running at the demon and swinging her Aventi at his head. The demon whipped his shield around in time to deflect her strike, but in doing so he lost his grip on the child and she tumbled toward the ground. In a blur of speed, Fallon vaulted over the seats, raced to the child and scooped her up in her arms, hugging her close to her chest. As fast as Fallon was, the Knight managed to nick her with the edge of his shield and she went flying through the air. She tucked into a protective ball around the child and bounced along the aisle in a violent roll.

"Lindsay!" the mother screamed.

Fallon jumped to her feet and pushed the mother toward the exit. "Go!" She just hoped Blane and Joseph would see them come out of the train at the back and take care of the demon. Once outside, she grabbed the elbow of the stumbling mother and led them at a run to a safe distance away from the wreckage. When she saw no sign of pursuit, she set the child on the ground. "You're safe now. Come on, sweetie, get up."

The child remained motionless.

Fallon dropped to her knees. "Come on, baby. Wake up." She patted her pale cheeks, but the girl's head rolled listlessly.

The mother fell down beside her. "Lindsay! Linds! What's wrong with her?" she asked, shaking the girl's shoulders.

Fallon rocked back on her heels. "I don't know...maybe the fall..."

"No...no!" The woman started to cry as she called her daughter's name over and over again.

Fallon stood. Through vision blurred by tears, she glanced back toward the train and saw Blane charge the demon and take a brutal hit to the chest. Somehow, he managed to stay on his feet and swung again with his Aventi. The Knight stepped in close, grabbed Blane by the wrist and struck him with a gauntleted fist. This time, Blane did fall and didn't move.

She glanced down at the bereaved woman. "I'm so sorry," she mumbled and took off to go to Blane's aid. A surge of white-hot fury propelled her forward in a mindless charge at the monster who killed an innocent child and was about to kill her friend. A scream of challenge tore from her throat at sight of the Black Knight poised over Blane.

The demon's helmeted face turned toward her and he stepped out to meet her. She watched for any sign of the wicked black lightning that he could pull from the ground, but by his stance he seemed eager for a close up confrontation.

Well, I'll give him one.

She knew her strikes couldn't penetrate the Knight's armor, so she aimed for a breach at the seam, right under his arm. Grunting with effort, she lunged. The Knight laughed, anticipating her move and knocked her strike wide. Fallon spun back, refusing to back down. Her sword whistled toward him once again and their blades met in the air with a crash of metal.

Where is Joseph?

Then, she saw him out of the corner of her eye, hunkered down over the dead girl who wasn't much smaller than he. He placed a hand on the child's forehead ignoring the agonized wails of the mother. Suddenly, a bright light burst from Joseph into the girl and her chest heaved up in an air-sucking gasp.

"Lindsay!" the mother cried. "Are you all right?" She took the child in her arms with a look of bewilderment at the retreating figure of the boy.

Fallon had no time to contemplate the Immortal's heroics as she ducked underneath another vicious swing of the Black Knight's shield.

When the Knight saw Joseph coming on, slowly, inexorably, he roared in defiance and ran at him. Joseph simply kept walking, calming taking his bow from his shoulder. Fallon stood there in frozen horror as the large menacing Knight sprinted toward the diminutive Immortal.

Fallon cried out, not sure what she could do to help.

Joseph drew back the bowstring and shot while he walked, never missing a step.

With contemptuous laughter, the Knight threw up his shield. But, the laughter was cut off when the rod of light penetrated his shield, armor and open mouth, and came out through the back of his head. The creature lit up in a blinding glow and vanished from sight.

Fallon stood spellbound.

From the ground, Blane groaned and sat up. "The Knight! Is he destroyed?"

"Yes," Fallon said, helping him to his feet. "We have Joseph to thank."

"And, several memories to erase," Blane observed wryly, noticing the people who stayed behind to watch the fight unfold.

Fallon waited for Joseph to approach. "How did you heal that child?" she asked when he neared.

Blue eyes twinkled. "Magic."

⚜

Tyras stared out of the window of his new study. Rain pelted the glass, casting his view of the world into a dim, gray replica of itself. The sun that Tyras longed to see had yet to make an appearance since his arrival. *My doing?* Quite possible. He supposed it was just as well. The brightness of this world already gave him a blinding headache, so the sun could very well prove unbearable should it decide to emerge from behind the clouds. Still, there were many beautiful things about the outside world that he wished to see again and would find a way to do so. *Soon. Very soon.*

He spun in the chair beneath him. "Stella! Stella!"

Within moments, a young, pretty woman in livery appeared at the door. The live-in housekeeper and nanny for the Monteros—the owners of the mansion—gave him a wide smile. Taken aback by the unusual gesture, Tyras hesitated for a moment, unsure. People did not smile when they looked at him. Ever.

"Yes, Mr. Smith?"

"Er...flowers."

"Flowers?"

"Yes, Stella, I...I would like fresh flowers delivered to this study on a weekly basis. With all the dreary rain, it would be nice to enjoy some color for a change."

She bowed her head. "Of course, Mr. Smith. I will pick them myself from the gardens."

He sniffed, deciding she was actually quite tolerable for a human. "Very well. I will have one of the guards escort you."

Her head twisted to glance uneasily at the sounds coming from a shadowy corner of the study. She backed away toward the door. "Is there anything else, Mr. Smith?"

"No, Stella, just the flowers."

The housekeeper turned and fled, almost falling in her haste to get out of the room.

Tyras lifted his feet and spun once again in the chair. *How delightful, making a chair that spins!* One of the many things about this world that was foreign to him. The advancements in medicine, science, communication and transportation were beyond his comprehension. Others were tantalizing in their simplicity—a hot bath, a beautiful woman to look upon, an exceptional drink. Tyras picked up his glass of cognac from the desk and sipped, humming in pleasure as the aged, fiery liquid slid down his throat.

"Master like drink?"

Tyras turned to Poati. The demon squatted in the corner and munched on a rat—still alive from the agonized squeals. Poati gave the rodent one last bite with his razor teeth and the screeching came to an abrupt halt.

Tyras had been very pleased to discover that his servant had managed to find a way out of the portal before the meddling angels of Emperica closed it again.

"Yes, Poati, I do like this drink very much."

"Master like girl?"

The image of Nicola's face came to his mind. Long auburn hair, big brown eyes, soft skin. His own Nicola had been dark of hair and eyes as well, and this girl reminded him of her very much. Her mannerisms, her fighting spirit. "Yes, I like the girl."

"Girl like Master?"

"No, Poati, girl does not like me very much at all, I'm afraid."

"Poati can make girl like Master."

"No, Poati, leave the girl to me."

A knock sounded outside of the office. "Enter."

Gordon Strand, his jowls looking more pronounced than before, walked into the room wearing what he had come to learn were army fatigues. Tyras didn't trust the man, but at the moment he very much needed him. It prickled at him to have to depend on anyone, but there was too much yet for him to learn before making any moves.

"The cells are ready in the lower level."

"Well done. Go ahead and move the Montero family down there until we need their bodies." Tyras stood, picked up his glass and moved around the desk. "What news do you have of the Emissiers, Strand?"

"All dead."

"Ah, wonderful news." That meant the Knights no longer had their communication link to Emperica. "Anything else?"

"Yes, I just received a report that one of the Black Knights has been killed."

Tyras set down his glass. "Really? A pity one was killed so soon, but they are here as diversions only." He looked back at Strand. "A Knight of Emperica?"

"Several."

"Yes, well, we will have to deal with them soon. Until then, I trust the remaining Black Knights will be able to keep the angels occupied while I pull my plans together. We need to start with the top leaders to help herd the sheep into their frightened huddles."

Strand tilted his head. "Humans may not be the sheep you think, Master, nor are they stupid. Even if the leaders are compromised, most will fight for their lives."

"Yes, but once they realize who it is they fight, they will back down. Their blinded eyes cannot comprehend what I am. They cannot stand against what I can do. It is all about attrition, Mr. Strand. Using the Black Knights and Kjin to whittle the field until the remainder lose their will to fight."

"Can...," Gordon's eyes strayed upward, "...the Creator do anything to stop you?"

"He will try. The final meeting between the two of us has been prophesized since the beginning of time."

"And...?"
"He will lose."

CHAPTER 6

Doorway to Freedom

Nikki rubbed her palms on her thighs as she paced. The digital clock on the dresser read three a.m. *Perfect.* There would be no better time to attempt an escape than the dead of night when vigilance would be at its lowest.

She stopped to glare at the door—the weakest point of her prison—as though if she looked long enough, she would be able see something beyond the sturdy oak. A Kjin stood guard outside and at every exit. The doctor already told her that. But, with the element of surprise, she might just stand a chance. Especially now that she felt fully recovered from the drugs she had been given.

Unless, of course, Tyras showed up out of thin air again, she reminded herself. Every time she thought about it, a chill raced up her spine.

I guess it's now or never. She shook out her hands and started to make her way toward the door, but then paused. Turning back to the room, she ran to a spare chair in the corner and broke one of the legs free with a crack of splintered wood. She hefted the broken piece in her hands. It was lighter than she hoped, but it would still do some damage with her strength behind it.

A creaking noise sounded behind her. She whirled around to the door. Bouncing on the balls of her feet, she poised her new club in the air and waited.

The door now stood ajar. But, no one came in. No sound came through the opening.

"Dr. Morris?" she called softly.

Silence.

Is someone helping me escape? She shook her head. No, something was off. No demon would leave his post and risk facing Tyras' anger. Her heart pounded in her chest. Club in hand, she made her way to the door and swung it open all the way, prepared to attack.

No one was there.

Cautiously, she peeked over the threshold into a carpeted, deserted hallway. A large, grand staircase descended to a lower level at the far end. Hugging the wall, she crept forward. Expecting a demon to jump out and stop her at any moment, she still kept going. She had to take a chance.

At the top of the staircase, she looked down at an empty, tiled foyer and unguarded front door. No Kjin stood watch like Dr. Morris told her there would be.

That's odd. Could she trust the doctor? The woman wasn't a demon, but she could have been coerced into making Nikki think she had no way out.

She licked her lips. Escape appeared to be within reach, but logic told her it couldn't be. Her gut told her if she went for that door, she would pay for it. But, if she *did* manage to make it outside, they would never catch her then.

Indecision rooted her feet beneath her. It had been a very long time since she had been this afraid. All peripheral vision receded to black and there was only the door. A way out that seemed miles away, but in reality just a few steps. She chastised herself for hesitating. *You are a warrior, Nikki Falco! Go!*

That single word impelled her down the stairs and in a sprint over the slick marble foyer. She crashed against the door and reached for the handle. Her heart soared when it turned in her hand.

It was unlocked!

A flash of red out of the corner of her eye was the only warning she had before a hard blow slammed her to the ground. The unexpected assault left her momentarily dazed, and she flinched in shock when a small body crawled on top of her and straddled her.

The little demon with his blonde curls looked surprisingly innocent, despite his red skin, and it made her hesitate. The creature used the delay to open his mouth and show her a bloody grin with strands of coarse hair stuck between his pointed teeth.

Before she could react, he bent down and sank his fangs into her neck. A scream tore from her as a burst of fire blossomed at her throat and spread through her chest. She tried to lift her arm to throw him off, but he scrambled away out of her reach. It wouldn't have mattered. She couldn't move a muscle. Whatever vile substance his bite contained paralyzed her. She could only lie there as the red monster circled her, making anticipatory clicking sounds with his tongue.

Then, he attacked.

He fell on her and started biting. Her legs. Her arms. Her face.

"No! Please, no!"

Each nip tore small chunks of flesh from her body. "Master will save you," the demon whispered. "Girl will like Master."

Another tormented scream echoed in her ears. It could have been the demon. More likely, it was her. Rivulets of blood striped her body, dripping to the cold tile beneath her. As the venom spread through her, the pain lessened, but the revolting sensation of the creature tugging at her skin remained and the sickening sounds of his butchery.

She willed her mind to a happier place, refusing to succumb to the panic that tried to crawl its way free. August Rand's face floated before her vision. She supposed it was natural to think of him since just seeing him on the news. He looked the same, his blue eyes as resolute as ever. August Rand liked to win. Whether sparring with other Knights in training or a simple game of darts. It's what made him such a great warrior.

But, she had been the recipient of more tender looks, too.

She flashed back to the summer of 1978. It was her third date with August and she was snuggled up under his arm as they cruised in his TransAm. He drove too fast for the winding roads San Francisco was known for, but he wanted to impress her. Instead of discouraging him, she pushed him to go faster, laughing like a lunatic and even sticking her body out of the window to sit on the ledge at one point.

Young, stupid, reckless. All three applied.

Then, the screeching sound of car brakes, the crunch of metal. Her body hit the windshield and she died instantly. She never really learned how and when August died and didn't see him again in Emperica until much later. By then, guilt and regret and childhood love had ceased to exist. They were simply two angel Knights on a mission.

I'd give just about anything to see him now though. Just one more time. In person. August Rand would put a stop to this demon hurting her. She was sure of it.

"Poati! Off!" rumbled a stern voice above her.

August?

The demon obeyed the command, scattering away from her with a disappointed squeak. Strong arms lifted her off the floor and pressed her against a hard, sweltering chest. *No, not August. Tyras.* She wanted to cringe away from the contact, but his embrace protected her flesh from the little demon. It stopped her torment. For that, she would endure the short conveyance to her room.

But, he didn't carry her to her room. He carried her to his.

A sound kick by Tyras sent the door to his room flying open. A nervous glance inside told her that it was actually a study, not a bedroom. *Thank goodness.* A desk and file cabinets lined one wall beneath a large picture window. A small sitting area with a sofa and two chairs faced a burning hot fireplace. Several vases around the room displayed dead, brown flowers, their brittle leaves hanging on by a whisper.

Tyras released her just inside the door and set her on her feet. "Can you stand?"

"No."

He swept her up once again and carried her to the sofa. "You'll be fine. Your angelic body will rid itself of the venom and heal your wounds."

Even as he made the claim, her fingers and toes started to tingle with life.

He pointed to a closed door on the other side of the room. "Would you prefer instead to lie in my bed while you heal?"

Lie in your bed, Tyras? Not a chance. A shudder ran through her and she shook her head.

Tyras laughed. "My bed should not frighten you so much. Unlike Poati, I do not bite."

She looked down at the wounds on her arms still bloody and raw. *They should be healing faster than this.*

"Next time that thing comes near me, I'll kill it," she snarled, but the words sounded weak even to her ears. The demon frightened her. More so even than Tyras.

"Poati? I can assure you that his intentions were good even if his methods were somewhat extreme."

"Good intentions? A demon? That's laughable."

"A demon can perform goodly acts that help advance a cause dear to him."

"You, devil, are *not* good."

"I am a creation of God."

Nikki wanted to kill him. "The Creator doesn't produce evil. You must have been good at one time before whatever rotted inside your chest turned you against your maker."

"I rebelled."

"Oh, yes, against the creation of man."

"Yes," he hissed in disgust. "What an insult to put rodents on the same level as angels. There were many who did not agree. Not just me."

"But, you were the first, weren't you, *Father of Lies*?"

He smirked. "Is that what they call me? It's quite ironic since I do not lie. If anything, I am brutally honest."

"Then, look around! Can you see the truth in front of you? This world rejects your very presence! Everything you touch spoils and dies."

His red eyes slid to the dead flowers. "Hmm...yes, I've noticed that. An illusory scheme of the Creator no doubt."

"No, it's you, Tyras. Your evil destroys the beauty of life." She thought of Dr. Morris aging before her eyes.

Tyras sighed heavily. "Since you seem fixed on this discussion, tell me, Nicola, is murder evil?"

"Of course it is."

"What if a mother kills a man attacking her child? Is murder then acceptable in that instance?"

"Yes, Tyras. Any reasoned person can see that."

"So murder is not always evil. *Intent* decides."

"What are you getting at?"

His face turned solemn. "My intentions at the time."

"Oh, I think they were crystal clear, devil. You tainted this world at the onset of its creation because you thought you were better than humans. You wanted to see them fall."

"Humanity fell because of their imperfections."

"Only because you tempted and lied and deceived them. I wonder how the world would be today had you not been created!"

His face contorted in anger and he swooped in close to her. "You better be grateful I *was* created, Nicola, as I am the only thing standing between you and Poati. As you well know, there are worse things than death. How about I prove that *truth* to you right now?"

Tyras' threat quivered tautly in the air between them, ready to snap at any second, at a single breath, the mere blink of an eye. Nikki's newly recovered muscles clenched in readiness for an attack.

But, it didn't come—the standoff broken by a knock on the door outside.

"Enter," Tyras commanded tersely, pulling away but his eyes never leaving hers.

"The food you requested, Master."

"Set it on the table and then go."

Nikki broke eye contact first to look at the Kjin at the door. He looked quite a bit older than the last time she had seen him working at The Blackstone, but she recognized Gordon Strand. *Is there any chance he will help me?* No. But, it showed her level of desperation to be looking to a Kjin for help over two demons from Mordeaux.

"You should eat quickly, Master, the eggs—"

"Go!"

Strand set the tray down on a small table and hurried out without a single glance in her direction.

"You should be able to walk now, Nicola. Come over and eat."

Does he really expect me to eat with him? She stood and tested her balance. "I'm not hungry."

In a flash of movement, he pinned her back against the sofa, his face inches from hers. "Enough games! You must decide now. Will you be my partner in the new world? Think quickly, Nicola. Power! Riches!"

Her body trembled violently in disgust.

He ran a blistering finger down her cheek, his smile carnal. "And, pleasure. I promise you, little angel, I will have you squirming with pleasure."

A sickened scream tried to force its way out of her throat, but her refusal came as a whisper between tightly clenched teeth. "Never."

His mouth pulled up in a grin. "Do you really think you have a choice? You *will* accept my offer, Nicola. You will be my wife."

"I'd rather marry a sewer rat."

Amusement faded back to anger. "I see now that it will take more convincing." He pushed away from her. "Strand!"

The door opened immediately.

"Yes, Master."

Tyras stalked away from her. "Take this woman to her room."

Gordon grabbed her arm in a vise-like grip and lifted her from the couch.

Backed turned away from them, Tyras picked up a glass of wine from the table. "Not her old room, Strand. Nicola will now be sharing living space with the Monteros."

Nikki snorted a small, victorious laugh before Gordon yanked her out of the room. "You can't touch me, Tyras!" she screamed. "I am cloaked in faith!"

Glass shattered against the closing door.

CHAPTER 7

Window to Freedom

Gordon pressed a gun to her back. "Get moving."

Nikki did as she was told, content at the moment in winning her first battle. *I must win the war, too. I can't let him break me.* "So, Gordie, where is your boss, Cesar Grant?"

"He didn't make it. Pissed off the wrong person."

"Is that so?" She glanced back at the gun in Gordon's hand. Not close enough. She'd have to find a better opportunity.

I won't give in!

She continued to repeat the mantra in her head as Gordon pushed her ahead of him. He opened a door to a set of stairs that led down into darkness. *This isn't good.*

"Go."

She stepped inside and they wound their way down into the bowels of the mansion. Four levels down, they came out into a musty hallway lit only by a single, bare light bulb. The Kjin pointed to an arched black iron door at the end of the short corridor. Nikki's heart skipped a beat. *A door that will be impossible to breach.* She realized with certainty that if she went through that door, her chances at escape would dwindle from negligible to non-existent. The time for better opportunities had vanished.

She shook her hands out and turned. "Hey, Gordie?"

The tall Kjin arched an eyebrow.

Her elbow came up swift and sure connecting with his nose, and she heard a hollow snap as the bone broke. Gordon screamed out in pain, his hands going up to his face. Nikki pushed by him and took off at a sprint for the stairs, knowing Gordon would never catch her now. *I can do this.*

She ran as fast as she could. The sounds of Gordon's heavy tread weren't far behind, but the turns on the staircase prevented him from getting a shot off at her.

I'll have to come back for Dr. Morris. As much as the thought disturbed her, it was the only way either one of them had a chance of survival.

As quietly as possible, she pushed open a door on the third floor, judging this as the level where the main entrance was located and hoping Strand would think she had continued up. She took off down the hallway and the door crashed open behind her.

Strand hadn't been fooled.

I just need a window! One without bars! She crashed through a door on the right and hurled herself across the room. *Yes!* Lunging toward the window, her fingers clawed their way underneath the bottom slat and pushed. Teeth gritted in panic, she inched the window up as fast as she could. Fully open now, cool air wafted over her face and nothing ever felt so good in her entire life. With no time to waste, she leapt up onto the sill at the same time a heavy object slammed into the back of her skull.

Instead of jumping forward to freedom, she fell back into darkness.

◈

Tyras watched the red wine slide down the closed door of the study and pool in a scarlet stain on the carpet. Taunting him. Admonishing him of the time he let slip away due to his preoccupation with Nicola. But, what an asset she would be to his cause! What a blow to the Creator to take one of his prized Knights as his own! A shiny token to parade about and prove *him* the victor.

He ran a finger absently along the table next to him and knew that if he looked down, he would see a blackened streak left by his touch. Nicola was right. This world did reject him. Fortunately, he wasn't asking for consent. *But, it would help*, he freely admitted.

Ultimately, the fight for earth would come down to him and his maker. A human war would solidify his position as ruler among the rats, but he would never be able to sit that throne until the final battle with

Emperica. That's why he needed Nicola. To act as his shield against the light. To cut down all those that would come against him while he fought the Creator.

And, this time would be different.

Unless, of course, the Creator decided to destroy the world again, but Tyras felt that scenario unlikely as he vowed never to do so again after the great flood. No, it would come down to a duel and he would have to be ready. He had the might of Mordeaux behind—or should he say beneath—him. The fires of hell were his to command even from here and he would bring them to bear against his enemy.

This world will be mine! He slammed his fist on the table and one of the vases with dead flowers toppled to the ground.

"Stella!"

Within moments, the housekeeper appeared. "Yes, Mr. Smith?"

"Flowers! I need flowers!" *Damnation! If I can't get the blasted flowers to accept me, how am I to capture a nation?*

She looked at the vases in confusion. "But, I brought fresh flowers in just this morning."

"You picked late bloomers, obviously. Do it again and do not fail me this time."

"Of course, I will get them right away."

"Leave me and send in Gordon Strand."

As she bowed herself out, Tyras picked up a map marked with key locations targeted for takeover. War should be at the forefront of his mind, but his thoughts drifted to big brown eyes, lush red lips and feminine curves. But, she was so much more than that. What dwelled inside the angel Knight captivated him even more. A passionate spirit. A woman who did not give up easily. A warrior who went bravely to battle for her beliefs. It pleased him that he could still appreciate these qualities. Somehow, he must get her to believe in *him*.

He almost laughed aloud at the absurdity. It had been a very long time since he cared what another thought of him. Too long to remember the sentiment, anyway. Mostly likely back when his heart was pure and he was in the good graces of the Creator.

He shook his head violently. That was then, this is now.

Gordon Strand opened the door. "Master?"

He swung his head to the door and frowned. "What happened to your nose?"

"The girl broke it trying to escape again."

The news annoyed him. *Why doesn't Nicola simply accept her fate?* He could get a hundred human women to fight each other to the death to be chosen as his mate! But, he didn't want a human. He wanted Nicola. A deep longing thrust its way through the blackened vestiges left by his rage. Not since *his* Nicola betrayed him had he felt any emotion close to this invigorating desire for the Knight. He wanted her. He *needed* her. "Where is she now?"

"In the cells."

"Leave her there until I'm ready for her." He pointed a finger down at the map and it burned a hole straight through to the table. "Billingsley should be here soon. After that, we'll need to travel to Camp Drexton. I want a firsthand look at this army he has created."

Strand's eyes lit up, anxious Tyras knew, to be on the field of battle. "I'll make the arrangements."

"Any news from the Kjin in the Secret Service detail?"

"No, but he should be with the President now."

"He needs to get inside that body immediately, Strand."

"That won't be a problem."

CHAPTER 8

A Change of Plans

The blast of a car horn caused Vincent to jerk the car hard to the left. "These people drive like morons!" the Immortal groused. "What are we, in a race? And, what's with all these gadgets?" he asked, waving his hand in front of the dashboard. "Come on. People can't roll up a window anymore?"

August smiled at Vincent's distress as he navigated the busy streets of Roanoke. The world had changed unbelievably since *he* was last here, and it had been even longer for the older Immortal. The pace of technology had always been a source of wonder to him, but he had no time to think about it now. Not with everything on his plate. The first of which was to get the President of the United States to safety. Things were about to get much worse before they got better and people would need a familiar figurehead to keep the panic to a minimum.

He pulled a photograph from his front pocket and rubbed a thumb over Nikki's face. He knew when he came back she wouldn't be here, but it still hurt. Like a sledgehammer to the gut. More so now back in his vulnerable human form than when he made the decision to return. Like Blane, he, too, hoped that Nikki was happily returned to Emperica and not at this very moment being tortured in the pits of Mordeaux. Eventually, though, he *would* learn the truth of her fate and if she was in the underworld, he would find a way to go after her. He let her down once before and wouldn't fail her again.

"What do you have there?" Vincent asked.

"Nothing," he mumbled and shoved the photo back in his pocket.

Vincent grunted but didn't pry. "Is that it?" he questioned jerking his chin forward.

August glanced out of the window and read the sign above the red-roofed restaurant. Pancakes Palace. "Yeah, that's it."

"We're meeting Sam Barnes at a pancake house? At night?" Vincent asked.

"Where else? If you don't expect to see someone in a particular place, you don't."

Horns honked again as Vincent veered into the right lane to pull into the parking lot.

"What's your problem? I had to make a turn!" he yelled out the open window at a rude gesture by one of the aggressive drivers. "You're lucky I don't take my whip to you!"

He pulled his head back in and noticed the look of surprise on August's face. "Did I just say that?" he asked, steering into a parking spot.

August nodded.

"These human emotions are all over the place! I can't help it!"

August laughed as he got out of the car. "Well, get it under control, because you're going to be here a very long time, my friend."

He led the way into the restaurant and spotted a bearded man in a corner booth discretely signaling to them. August slid into the seat next to the Secret Service Director and made introductions. "The President?" he asked Sam.

"He'll be here in a few minutes, enough time for us to plan this thing. I'll be honest, I haven't talked to an Emissier in a very long time, so I was pretty disturbed by the message I received. Is *he* really here?"

"Yes, he is."

Sam rubbed a hand down the fake, but incredibly realistic, hair on his jaw.

"Vincent and I will personally escort you and the President to the bunker, but once we know he's safe, we'll have to leave. I have an old score to settle with a couple of demons from Mordeaux."

"Demons, too?"

"The worst kind. Fallen angels."

Sam whistled. "How long do you think it's going to take to deal with these demons and Tyras? At this point, I've only told the President that an attack on his person is imminent. Although, he knows what I am and what we're dealing with here, he won't sit still for too long. He'll need more answers."

"Give me a few days. A week would be better. I'll have to press on some demon flesh pretty hard to get Tyras' location, but even if I'm unsuccessful I think the devil will make himself known before long. He thrives on the attention. On the fear."

Sam nodded toward the window. "There's the President now." August took notice of the black Escalade with tinted windows pulling into the parking lot. "We'll head straight to the airport from here."

"Let's go, then," August said and followed Sam out of the Pancake Palace. "Who's in the car?"

"The President and two agents. The Vice President and First Lady are already on board AF1. Other cars with agents are spread out over the area."

Vincent took the lead and arrived at the vehicle first. He pulled opened the door. The surprised look on his face confirmed what August's Kur was already telling him.

A Kjin was in the car with the President.

"Damn it!" Sam barked, his Kur warning him of the same.

Vincent didn't hesitate. He reached into the car, grasped the forearm of the President of the United States, and yanked him bodily out of the car. Sam caught him while screaming for aid into some hidden device on his collar.

August jumped into the car and screamed "Go!" to the driver, hoping he wasn't the Kjin. He wasn't. It was the one in the back. As August turned, a knife jabbed toward his face and he jerked back just in time.

"What the hell is going on?" the driver yelled.

"Just drive!" August shouted back, catching the lurching Kjin by the throat. "The President is in danger from this man. Radio Sam Barnes if you have to, but drive!"

The driver stepped on the gas sending August and the demon slamming into the floorboard in a tangled heap. Finding it hard to get his legs underneath him for leverage, August grabbed the Kjin by the shirt front and hurled him up over his head, directly into the reinforced glass window of the Escalade. Blood spray from the demon's ruined nose splattered the window. Two small, white objects fell from his howling mouth. His two front teeth as it turned out.

The knife swiped down at August again and managed to catch him this time in the flesh below his shoulder. White, hot pain bloomed in his arm, but he ignored it and seized the Kjin's wrist in a two-handed grip. As they struggled for position, August let go to grab the wallet sticking out of the demon's inside jacket pocket and tossed it to the floor. The Kjin wouldn't be needed it where he was going, but August might.

"Where to?" the driver questioned, having apparently gotten through to Sam.

August roared with effort and heaved with all his super strength sending the Kjin sprawling into the back seat. "Doesn't matter. This won't take long." August unfolded himself from the floor and shifted into wraith form.

"What...what's going on?" the driver asked, his eyes wide in the rear view mirror.

The demon's eyes went just as wide.

August unsheathed his dagger and slithered to the back seat. He wrapped a vaporous arm around the Kjin's throat and slid the weapon between his ribs. For a brief second, the demon's body lit up in a flare of white and then disappeared.

"What the hell? What's going on?" the driver demanded.

August ducked behind the seat and shifted back into human form. He popped his head up. "We're all set, he's down," he assured the driver.

"What was that light? Some kind of new weapon? If so, I want one."

"I'll talk to Sam," he said noncommittally.

"Hey, I can't even see that guy. You got him crammed in good back there."

August ignored him and picked up the wallet from the floor. No photos, no mementos. A few hundred dollars and a single piece of paper. He pulled it out and read. Next, he dug out his cell phone and called Vincent. "Is the President safe?"

"Yeah, but we're long gone."

"That's fine because I won't be able to join you after all. There's been a change of plans."

∽

Blane hung up his phone.

"Where to now?" Fallon asked.

"Camp Drexton in Sandoville," Blane answered.

"Sandoville?"

"The research team in Reglan still doesn't have anything concrete on the location of the third Knight, so August wants us to head to Drexton to see what we can learn about those helicopters that were used in the attacks a few weeks back. He wants to know if the Kjin simply stole the birds or if the demons have actually infiltrated the military base there."

"Well, we've suspected General Nash and Governor Billingsley for some time now."

"Yeah, it doesn't look good for those two."

"Is August still with the President?"

"No, he had a run in with a Kjin and found an address in the demon's pocket that he wants to follow up on and then he'll meet us in Sandoville."

"All right. Let's drive a couple of hours and then we should find somewhere to sleep," Fallon said.

"The car?"

She whipped around to face him. "You're lucky I can't reach your forehead. Sleep in the car? No way. I need a few hours of decent sleep and a hot shower or I'll be of no use to anyone." She eyed the stubble on his chin. "Neither will you."

Joseph made an amused snort from the back seat.

"Fine," Blane said, rubbing a hand over his face. "We'll get a room somewhere."

"Smart move," Joseph observed.

Blane looked in the rear view mirror. "Uh, no comments from the peanut gallery back there."

Joseph just laughed again.

Fallon took out her phone and scrolled through her texts. "Have you heard from Juliet?"

Blane shook his head. "No, she hasn't answered any of my calls which is weird and kind of scary."

"Kade hasn't answered me either. I wonder if he's still mad about not being able to come along."

Blane glanced at her sideways and saw her hand go to her stomach, something he'd seen her do often today, but he waved her comment away. "Kade and Juliet know exactly what they married into. They'll be fine."

For some reason, the kid in back snorted again.

"Oh, are you an expert on relationships, Immortal?" Blane asked.

The boy quickly shook his head. "Far from it. Humans amaze me all the time."

"So, what's your story, Joseph? Why are you here?"

Blane watched the Immortal shrug in the mirror. "A few reasons. Mainly, I came because I'm the best archer in Emperica." He tilted his head self-consciously. "I hope that doesn't sound too arrogant."

"No, I've seen you shoot. I just wish there was some way you could get back home at some point."

"Are you looking forward to going back?" the boy asked.

Blane thought of Juliet, Teddy and Georgie. "Yes, in good time. Right now, I'd really like to explore this second chance I have."

"With your family?" the Immortal guessed.

Blane smiled. "Yes. They mean everything to me. I'd do anything to protect the life I have with them."

"Ah, the second reason I'm here."

Chapter 9

Tyras Courts

Nikki came awake slowly, the knot in the back of her head throbbing painfully, reminding her that this was the second time her skull had been bashed since she had been in Tyras' custody. She squinted into the darkness. The black bars confirmed what she feared. Her new room was a prison cell. Probably behind that black iron door.

Gingerly, she sat up and scanned her surroundings. There wasn't much to see. A single cot and toilet. Beyond the cell were three more just like hers—an empty one to the left and two more across the hallway. The shadowy gloom prevented her from seeing if they were occupied.

She glanced down at her arms and legs and the gouges left by the demon, Poati. If her limbs looked this bad, she wondered what her face must look like. She doubted she would ever heal fully so near to Tyras' destructive aura.

Or, get the chance to escape again.

Despair rounded her shoulders and she pulled her knees in tight to her chest on the cot. *I'm not afraid to die, but it hurts to know that I won't be able to help Blane and Fallon. That I won't get to see August again.* The short time they shared together suddenly all the more coveted in the wake of the reality that it would never be.

"Hello?"

Nikki scooted off the cot and ran to the bars. A man, woman and little girl stood locked in the cell across from hers. "You must be the owners of this house," she said, speaking her thought aloud.

The man nodded and pulled his daughter close. "Who are you?"

"My name is Nikki."

"I'm Jacob Montero and this is my wife, Sheila, and our daughter, Claire."

She gave the girl a sad smile. "It's kind of scary down here, isn't it?"

Claire's lip quivered and she nodded. "But, it wouldn't be so bad if I had Lucy with me."

"Lucy?"

"My doll."

Nikki recalled the dresser with all the dolls on top. "Which one?"

"She has dark hair with a white ribbon and wears a blue dress."

"Oh, yes, I think I know her."

The girl's eyes grew as big as saucers. "How do you know, Lucy?"

"I saw your bedroom when I was upstairs."

"Do you think you can get her for me?"

"Honey..." the mother said, gently reproving her daughter's outrageous request.

"I'll do my best, Claire," Nikki promised just as her hearing picked up footsteps on the stairs outside of the door. "Someone is coming," she whispered, with a pointed look at Jacob. "Keep your family quiet and out of sight."

Jacob shuffled his family back into the corner of the cell.

Nikki waited, anticipating Strand or another Kjin with water or a meal, but it wasn't either. It was Tyras.

He came through the door and walked to her cell, filling her vision with his large frame. For a long moment, he just stared at her. Then, he cleared his throat as though nervous. "Will you walk with me?"

Walk? To my execution? On a moonlight stroll? What are you asking? And, do I really have a choice? No. Any possible chance at escape existed outside of this cage. She could do nothing for herself or the others locked away down here.

"Yes. I'll walk with you."

Red eyes glowed with...*delight?* He produced a key from his pocket and opened her cell door. "After you."

Nikki walked out, sparing a brief glance in the cell across the way. The family had taken her advice and seemed to have disappeared. Without a word, she went ahead of Tyras and started to climb the stairs. He stopped her at the third level.

"There's a small art gallery on this floor that I thought you would enjoy." *I'd enjoy my freedom a whole lot more, Tyras. Exactly two seconds after your death.*

Nodding, she went through the door and after a short walk down a highly-polished, hardwood hallway, they entered a large studio. Beautiful art of various styles lined high white walls beneath halogen lights. White modern furniture and a marble floor with gold inlay gleamed with opulence. The Monteros were obviously very well off. A family used to this much space and luxury could not be coping well in a tiny cell.

Despite herself and her circumstance, Nikki breathed, "Gorgeous."

Tyras brushed by her to view one of the paintings. "I thought you might like it."

His response brought her back to reality. "Do you take all your prisoners on strolls to enjoy good art?"

He sighed heavily and turned to her. "Don't you understand, Nicola? I don't want you as a prisoner. I want you in my life of your own free will." He ran an agitated hand through his white hair. "I don't know why that's important to me, but it is."

"I am a Knight of Emperica, Tyras! You are...the devil. How can those two things mesh? Ever?" *I can't believe I'm entertaining this.* "Just let me go."

"I can't do that," he said and stalked a few feet away. "You remind me of someone," he said softly.

"Well, I'm not her."

"I know."

"You really loved her, didn't you?" she asked in bewilderment. Whatever caused Tyras to turn out the way he did, he hadn't always been that way. It gave her hope that if she spent enough time with him, she may be able to convince him to let her go. And, she wouldn't leave without Dr. Morris and the Monteros.

"Yes."

"Was she one of the original twelve angels like you?"

"Yes." He waved off further questioning. "But, enough of this inane chatter. Your choices remain the same. You will either be my wife or you will return to Emperica. Which will it be?"

Stall, Nikki! "Can I have a day or two to think about it?"

"You are trying my patience, Nicola, but I will allow you the day and night to decide. By tomorrow morning, I will have your answer."

"And, you will," she told him, grateful for any delay no matter how small.

He nodded and pulled cuffs of lace through the sleeves of his coat. "I'm afraid I have business to attend to. I will escort you back to your cell now."

"Wait! Can I go upstairs and get something out of my old room first?"

He shrugged. "I suppose. No games, Nicola."

Nikki hurried out of the studio and back to the stairwell before Tyras changed his mind. On the fourth floor, she easily found Claire's room and went in. The medical equipment used to keep her alive was still there and it made her wonder where Dr. Morris was.

"Hurry, Nicola, I have things to do," Tyras admonished from the doorway.

Nikki went to the dresser lined with dolls and found the one with the blue dress. "I'm ready."

Tyras' eyebrows rose in surprise. "Interesting selection. I would have thought you far too old for that kind of thing."

She walked by him without commenting and he didn't press.

In silence, they made their way back to her cell and he wasted no time locking her back in. "One day, Nicola. That is all. I will return for your answer in the morning."

∾⊙

August toweled his hair dry and studied his reflection in the foggy bathroom mirror. It had been many decades since he last saw this mug. He rubbed a hand down the stubble on his jaw. Nikki always asked him not to shave. Said it made him look tough. Well, since he didn't have anything to shave with, stubble it would be no matter what it made him look like.

Nikki.

It wasn't surprising that she filled so many of his thoughts. Even before the battle at Baylor's Pass, Darius started prepping him to return to earth and had no problem using Nikki as incentive. "You've loved her your whole life," Darius told him. "She's down there and she needs you." For an Elder, he sure knew how to manipulate someone to get what he wanted.

Nikki.

He would give anything right now to have her walk through the bathroom door and tease him. To wrap her arms around his neck and kiss him like she used to do. To this human body of his, it was only yesterday that they were together, not thirty years. This body remembered quite vividly the feel of her soft skin. The sight of her red lips. The smell right at the base of her throat.

He grunted in pain and looked down. *Hmm...it's been a long time since that's happened.*

Nikki.

He slammed his fist on the bathroom sink and spun away from the mirror. *I need to stop thinking about Nikki! She's lost to me!* In more ways than one. She would never return to earth again and he could never leave. And, even if she were here, it's not like she would remember anything about their love. A Ha'Basin over thirty years ago stripped her of every memory they ever shared together.

Hastily wrapping the towel around his waist, he left the bathroom and grimaced when he saw a cockroach run across the bedroom floor. This rundown motel looked a whole lot better last night then it did now. He grabbed his jeans off the bed and stepped into them, praying they were free of insects.

Once dressed, he walked to the bed and picked up one of two items on the nightstand—the photo of Nikki.

Using the palm of his hand, he tried to flatten out the beating it took during his fight in the Escalade. When he was satisfied it was as smooth as it was going to get, he put it back into his pocket and picked up the other item, a white piece of paper with a single address. Any Kjin working in a plot to transform the President of the United States had to be pretty high up in the demon hierarchy—if there was such a thing. He hoped the trail would lead him to Tyras, but even if it turned out to be a hive of commanders, it would be worth the diversion just to take them out.

But, if he *could* get to Tyras and put this whole thing down without any more bloodshed, all the better. *If* being the key word. Would he be able to get close enough? Could he even defeat Tyras if he got the chance? Would his dagger be effective against the devil?

Darius had been uncertain when questioned.

August was even more so.

Chapter 10

Camp Drexton

A military post that should have been busy with soldiers going about their duty looked deserted. Fallon propped her elbows in the dirt and adjusted the focus of her binoculars in on the building a hundred yards away. *Where is everyone?* Blane, pressed up tight against her right side, nudged her arm, so she handed him the binoculars. Joseph, lying on her left side, simply watched the abandoned base without expression. Something she was coming to expect from the little Immortal.

They were sprawled over the top of an earthen bunker that she assumed the National Guard used for training purposes. A low stone wall, bolstered with heavy sand bags ran a good quarter mile on either side, and a large, open-sided wooden structure with a roof stood just a few feet away.

Fallon felt another twitch between her shoulder blades. Even though the bunker did its job of keeping them hidden from the front, their backs were completely exposed. Every minute or so, she threw a quick glance over her shoulder, but the area behind them remained clear.

"Think we should go in?" Blane asked. He wiped the rain off the binoculars and handed them to Joseph.

"Something is obviously not right here," Fallon answered. "Maybe we should wait for August and Vincent."

Blane reached over her back to pat Joseph's shoulder. "We got the archer here. That's all we need."

Whatever thoughts Joseph had on the matter, he didn't share with the two of them, but Blane seemed intent on investigating regardless.

"I guess it couldn't hurt to take a look," she admitted, although the encounter with the Black Knight at the train crash site paraded across her mind. *Yes, it could hurt. A lot.* "Let's make it quick. A fight with innocent soldiers is not what we're looking for."

That's all Blane needed to hear. He got up into a crouch and started forward keeping low to the ground. Joseph followed, running behind Blane's large bulk. Fallon waited a few seconds before joining in single file to keep their profile as narrow as possible. She removed her sweatshirt as she went to make sure her Kur was unobstructed.

"What's that?" Joseph asked.

Fallon peered around him. A figure in fatigues waved from the side of one of several green military jeeps on the tarmac between them and the building. Without a second thought, Blane veered toward him.

"Are you here to help?" the man asked when they approached. He was very young, maybe even a teenager still.

"Help with what?" Blane asked him.

"It's crazy. Some of the guys flipped out and locked up General Nash. Said it's on the orders of Governor Billingsley and they're waiting for him to arrive. They won't let anyone in or out of the training center over there." He pointed to the long, two-story building they had been watching.

That's interesting, thought Fallon. *We had always assumed General Nash was Kjin.*

"How many are involved with sequestering the General?" Blane asked.

Fallon understood the question. The answer would be the number of demons inside.

"I would say half, so probably a hundred. Heavily armed. Took us all by surprise. I was lucky enough to get out, but I haven't seen anyone else."

Blane turned back to her and Joseph. "Obviously, there's no time to wait for the other Immortals. We have to free the soldiers."

"I agree," Fallon said, taking her Aventi into her fist.

"Can you show us a way in?" Blane asked the young soldier.

"Yes, follow me."

They took off at a jog using the military vehicles on the tarmac as cover. "What's your name?" Fallon asked as they ran.

"Brad Murphy."

"Is everyone in one location?"

"Pretty much. Right in the main hall. I'll take you in the back way."

The soldier guided them around obstacles to the side of the building. After rounding the corner, Fallon slammed her back against the wall. The Kur on her arm ignited in a hot burn. "There are a whole lot of Kjin in there," she whispered.

Joseph took his bow in his hands.

"On three, we'll go in," Blane told them. "One, two...three."

Blane's boot connected with the knob and the door swung open and hit the inside wall.

Fallon followed Blane and Joseph in, Aventi unlit but held out in front of her. High windows on the second level of an open skywalk that ran along the perimeter of the building provide some illumination, but it took a moment to register what her eyes were telling her. It was empty. *Where are the soldiers?*

Despite her concern, she took a few steps forward. Her soft footfalls sounded loud in the cavernous room. No one was in sight—either human or Kjin, yet Fallon felt their presence all around her. Something wasn't right here. The solider insisted that...

The door clicked shut behind her and she spun around.

Said soldier was gone.

"It's a trap," Blane hissed.

"Of course, it is," Joseph commented.

"When did you know?"

"When we first saw the soldier. I did not sense any of the nervousness that should have accompanied his story."

"Why didn't you say something?"

"You said you wanted in. We're in."

"A little more thought-sharing would be appreciated."

The boy simply shrugged.

Movement above drew Fallon's attention. She stumbled back against Blane as figures in black glided down from the skywalk on ropes and herded the three of them together into the center of the hall.

In hindsight, she wished they had let Joseph take a good majority of the demons out with that remarkable bow of his before committing themselves inside, but they didn't and it was too late now.

She slammed her Aventi against her bicep and rushed to close with the nearest Kjin.

"Ah!" Her feet swept out from under her as a large net scooped her and the others into the air. The top of the net pulled closed as tight as a clam and smashed the three of them together, jostling with elbows and knees to get into an upright position.

The Kjin stood underneath the net looking up, one holding a gun to the head of Brad Murphy. "Stay where you are or the soldier bites it."

❦

Nikki's eyelids finally surrendered to the mental exhaustion of confinement. They continued to drift lower despite her attempts to stay awake. Her body felt lighter. Her fears faded away. *Anywhere, but here,* her mind whispered before preparing to whisk her away to where dreams are made.

The sound of the iron door opening jerked her back to full awareness in an instant. Alert now, she sat up on her cot in time to watch Gordon Strand shove an elderly woman into the cell next to hers. The push sent the woman to her hands and knees with a pitiful cry.

The demon locked the cell and turned and left without a word or backward glance.

"Are you all right?" Nikki asked and hurried to the bars that separated their two cells.

The figure on the ground stiffened and lifted her head to Nikki's voice. "I think so."

Concern for the old woman coursed through Nikki. *Where did she come from? How did she end up in this house of horrors?*

The woman slowly got to her feet, shuffled close and grasped the bars with yellowed, gnarled fingers. An ancient face, wrinkled with age peered up at Nikki.

She gasped. There was no mistaking those light amber eyes.

Dr. Morris.

"Oh, no," she moaned. A lump formed in her throat at the thought of how desperately this woman just wanted to get home to her children. And, now...her children would never recognize her. A worm of guilt wiggled into Nikki's conscience that she had not been able to save her. She reached through the bars to take hold of the doctor's wrists. "I'm so sorry, Dr. Morris."

"What's happened to me?" the doctor asked and began to weep.

"We're the prisoners of some very bad people, Dr. Morris." What else could she say?

"But, I'm old! I'll never see my children again. Oh, my poor babies!" She began to whimper, the pain too much to bear.

Nikki never felt more helpless in her life. "I...I wish there was something I could do."

"My body is giving out on me. I'm dying!"

With those last words, the decision came easy. Maybe there was something she could do after all. If Dr. Morris truly was dying, Nikki could at least try and make her final days as peaceful as possible. "Sit down. I'd like to share something with you."

The doctor wiped her tears with the back of her hand and nodded.

Sitting on the cold, hard cement with their hands clasped together, Nikki told Dr. Morris about Emperica.

In reverent whispers, she described colors so vivid they didn't seem real. Green grass that felt alive beneath bare feet. Blue waterfalls that mesmerized with their striking clarity and immense power. White silky clouds that soothed and embraced the soul with a life of their own.

She promised Dr. Morris an eternal life of peace and tranquility, and a pair of magnificent wings that would make her cry with joy at every buoyant step. People she had lost would be there to greet her. Her angelic life would be one of purpose and harmony. And, she would know love on a visceral level to which there was no frame of reference on earth.

Nikki knew she wasn't giving Emperica proper justice with her words, but the pain on Dr. Morris' face seemed lessened. Her shoulders a little straighter.

"Do you really believe all that?" the doctor asked in a soft voice.

"I've lived it."

Dr. Morris didn't say what she thought of that statement, and a companionable silence descended between them then, both lost in their own thoughts of the afterworld.

Suddenly, the doctor swung her gaze toward the corridor. "Oh, no," she whined in fright.

"What?" Nikki asked, her adrenaline kicking in.

"It's that thing!"

Nikki's blood ran cold when she heard the skittering of clawed feet stop at her cell. She backed away slowly.

Poati.

She swallowed at sight of him and stood as still as possible. *Maybe he won't come in.* For long terrifying moments, the demon just stood there and stared at her. Then, his hand came up to the lock of her cell. With a key.

"Get away!" Dr. Morris screamed.

The key turned in the lock. Poati stepped in and shut the door behind him, locking them both inside.

Nikki's heart pounded against her ribcage. *I can't let him bite me. I just have to wear him out. I'm bigger than him. And, faster.*

Poati grinned, showing his pointed teeth to her, devoid this time of the blood and hair.

She searched the room for a weapon, finally deciding on the only thing available to her. She pulled the single, thin sheet off the cot and wrapped both ends around her hands.

Poati lunged at her, but she caught him in the sheet and wrapped him up tight. She yanked the two sides together and flung him with all her strength against the cement wall of her cell. The little demon fell to the ground, but quickly got back up and attacked again. Nikki managed to stay out of his reach by a hairsbreadth as he chased her around the small area. She had no offense against his hardened, red scales! Her fists were useless, barely nudging the demon with every powerful blow she hammered at him.

"Nikki, here!"

She sprinted to the bars she shared with Dr. Morris, and the doctor pressed a surgeon's scalpel into her hand. "Go for the eyes," the doctor hissed.

"Thanks." Nikki pushed away from the bars and grabbed the sheet off the floor. All she had to do was wrap him up one more time and if not kill him at least blind him. "Come here, Poati," she goaded. "I have something for you."

He charged her and she swiped the scalpel at his face. The demon ducked underneath her swing, and the movement spun her off balance. Her arms windmilled as she stepped backward onto the edge of the sheet still dangling from her hand. Poati took advantage and tackled her the rest of the way to the ground.

"Nikki!"

She heard Dr. Morris' warning but it was too late. It had always been too late. Poati opened his cruel little mouth and bit into her neck. She lost feeling in her upper body immediately, the demon poison filtering through her veins. Her legs kicked uselessly in protest until they, too, became incapable of nothing more than the weak drumming of her heels on the concrete floor.

Poati continued to bite. Over and over again. Just like before. He didn't drink the blood—he seemed intent solely in her torture.

"Oh, Nikki," Dr. Morris moaned. "Get off her, you brute!"

When it felt like Poati had chewed every available space of flesh she owned, he got off her and left the cell.

Through the lethargy of blood loss, she heard the cell next door open and then the screams of Dr. Morris. From her peripheral vision, she saw Dr. Morris scramble under her small cot. Poati caught her ankle in his hand and dragged her free.

Then, he started in on her.

Every cry felt like a spike in Nikki's heart. Each scream more painful than the next. Dr. Morris wouldn't last long. She didn't have the healing powers that Nikki had.

And, she no longer had her scalpel to defend herself.

Chapter 11

Shields

The little demon came to her cell twice more during the day. More bites of paralyzing venom just when she started to regain movement. Enough of the punctures to drain her blood and keep her weak. Worse, he positioned her on her side so every time she opened her eyes, the corpse of Dr. Morris filled her vision.

The smell of death hung in the air, threatening to choke her at every breath. Despite the fetid aroma, hunger and thirst clawed at her insides, demanding to be sated. She couldn't remember the last time she had water and dehydration started to cloud her mind.

In one befuddled moment, she thought she saw Blane and Fallon hacking away at her cell in an attempt to free her. Hope soared in her until a small sniffle from Claire across the aisle caused the apparitions to vanish. In another fantasy, August Rand reached through the cell bars for her. Beckoning. His tattooed arm urging her to get up and save herself. Expending what little energy she could muster, she lifted an arm and stretched it toward August. *Take my hand, August! Get me out of here!* Her fingertips quivered as she stretched, farther and farther. But, he, too, dissolved when she blinked the blood from her eyes.

Now, she lay in a dazed fugue. Her body convulsed with shivers as the cement floor robbed her of warmth and set her teeth chattering inside her skull. *It's so cold.* Then, she remembered the sheet. Grumbling with effort, she flopped a deadened arm behind her to search the floor, but couldn't find it. A frustrated screech worked its way out of her.

"Are you all right, Nikki?"

The sudden voice startled her. "What...who's there?"

"It's me. Claire."

Claire? Oh, yes, the Montero girl. All of a sudden, it dawned on Nikki that the Monteros hadn't aged the way Dr. Morris had. Most likely because they hadn't been in Tyras' presence as much as the doctor. In their case, being locked away in this cell was a blessing.

Until the demons need their bodies.

"I'm fine, Claire."

"Did you get my doll?"

Nikki tried to laugh, but it came out as a snorting cough. "Yes, Claire, I did. Hang on." If she accomplished nothing else in this life, she *would* give this child her doll. "It might take a little bit," she said and willed her body to move.

"Did you get hurt? Daddy covered my ears after I heard you scream."

Using muscles that felt like jelly, Nikki inched herself closer to the cot. "I'm okay now."

"Good."

Nikki spotted the doll on the floor where it must have fallen when she grabbed the sheet. She extended her arm, praying that Poati would not come back yet.

Where she was freezing just moment ago, now sweat beaded her forehead. *Just another few inches.* Dragging her body by her forearms, she reached out once again and cried out in relief when her fingers finally snagged the little blue dress. "I have it, Claire!"

The girl clapped her hands in delight.

Feeling a bit stronger from the exertion, Nikki managed to roll over and toss the doll over to the other cell.

Claire quickly reached though the bars to scoop it up into her arms. "Thank you so much, Nikki! Oh, Lucy," she said, hugging the doll tight. "I've missed you."

A smile spread across Nikki's face. *My last good deed. I've done what I can here, but my time is up. If Tyras thinks he is breaking me, he is wrong. I welcome the bites, the cold and the pain. It means I'm one step closer to home.*

◈

Is this bloody rain ever going to stop? It was a thought Tyras had often as the incessant deluge pounded the window outside of his study. It made him idly wonder what the humans made of this rain that would not stop. All he knew was that he was sick to death of it. All of it. The gray clouds that roiled continuously above his head, the spoiled food, and the humans and Kjin alike who aged before his eyes. He told Nikki that he thought it merely a trick of the Creator, but he no longer believed that to be true. She was right. It was his fault. The tear that the fallen angel made in the fabric of the world to open the portal released some of the poison of Mordeaux into the atmosphere. Unfortunately, this indiscriminate taint that touched every aspect of life troubled him as much as the humans and he had no idea how to change it.

He tapped his chin in thought. Trying to see the world as Nicola saw things naturally caused him to revaluate his way of thinking. He came to earth to conquer and still intended to do so, but maybe it was possible to preserve the life here. Many years ago, he let his anger and greed and jealously shred Mordeaux into a wasteland of fire and brimstone. Let it feed his fury. Let his desire to be everything the Creator was *not* consume him. Become him. But, did he really want the mistakes of the past to follow him here? Could he even recover some of the virtues of his angelic beginnings?

For Nicola, he could at least try.

He twirled his chair toward Gordon. "Do you think I can change, Strand?"

The Kjin jerked awake, his once virile body now bent with age. "Master?"

"Do you think I can change? Try to be a better man."

Strand stared at him, his rheumy eyes focused now. "Change? Why would you want to do that?"

"I don't think Nicola will have me as I am. I believe I'll have to make changes to keep her." Tyras reached out and fingered the fresh flowers Stella brought in moments ago and they crumbled to dust at his touch. "I don't believe the world will have me as I am either. I wonder if I could actually make nice with the rodents."

"Why do you care what a sanctimonious angel thinks of you?"

"That, my friend, is a good question and one for which I do not have an immediate answer." *I only know that the hardened lump in my chest that serves as a heart beats a little faster every time I'm near her.* "Regardless, have arrangements been made for our trip to Camp Drexton?"

"Yes. Two cars will take us and the five Kjin here. They're good soldiers, so I don't want to leave them behind."

"No, no, they should go." Tyras eyed Strand with a scowl. "Why the bloody hell are you still in that body? You need a new one soon or it will be too late. Why don't you take the man in the cells?"

"Yes, it's time. I'll do it tonight."

A Kjin knocked on the door and peeked his head in. "Billingsley is here."

"Send him in."

The well-dressed and handsome governor of...*somewhere southwest*...strode into the room. He had dark hair with strands of gray at the temples and appeared slim and fit. He wore an arrogant tilt to his lips, but was smart enough to give the appropriate deference by bowing at the waist before Tyras. "Master."

"Billingsley. Have you had any word about the President?"

The governor paled slightly. "He got away and is beyond our reach at the moment."

Tyras narrowed his red eyes in anger. "Got away? You fool!"

"It wasn't my fault, Master, it was the Kjin that Strand sent!"

Gordon started to defend himself, but Tyras cut him off and started to pace. "Now, what? I really wanted the..." he wiggled his fingers in the air, "...black house!"

"Er...it's actually the white house."

He stopped in front of the governor. "Well, I'll make it black! There are no words for your incompetence, Billingsley."

"Camp Drexton is ours completely."

"As it should be since it is under your jurisdiction! But, it's in the middle of nowhere. I want every military base on the east coast under Kjin control within the week."

Billingsley's jaw dropped. "That's impossible, Master. It will take more time than that."

"Time I do not have! I need an army. I don't care how you do it, but I want all rodents east of..." he snapped his fingers in a prompt, "...what's that river again?"

"The Mississippi?"

"Yes, I want every rodent east of the Mississippi marching to my tune. If they resist, kill them."

"Yes, Master."

Somewhat mollified, he said, "We're leaving for Drexton in the morning. Will you travel with us?"

The governor shook his head, the relief on his face evident. "No, I'll be taking a flight back tonight."

"Very well. Dismissed."

As soon as Billingsley left, Tyras stalked to the door. He told Nicola he wouldn't see her until tomorrow, but he wanted to let her know that they would be leaving in the morning.

He left the study without the slightest thought that her answer might be no.

⚜

Nikki looked up in surprise when Tyras walked into the cell room. *Did he change his mind? Does he want his answer now instead of tomorrow?* At least she felt healed enough to be on her feet and wouldn't have to spar with him from the floor.

He stopped at the cell that held Dr. Morris' body. "I see Poati got a little overzealous."

The comment boiled her blood and she wanted nothing short of his death. Right then and there.

"Overzealous? That's how you describe the cold-blooded slaughter of a human being?"

"She was dying anyway, Nicola."

"Because of you!"

He walked to her cell and crossed his arms. "I did not come here to fight with you, but I grow so weary of your sermonizing. You wear your virtue like a mantle, Nicola, just daring others to try and knock it off so you can prove yourself better."

"You're wrong," she countered. "I don't wear it, it wears me. Just as your evil wears you. It oozes from your every cell. And, to think I almost convinced myself that you could be redeemed! Thankfully, my virtue shields me from your deceit."

"You hide behind it because you're weak!"

"I'm far from weak," she scoffed, choosing to ignore that fact that she faced him from behind *his* bars.

Tyras' features grew animated, the most she had seen from that rock of a face. "You came back to earth as you were created, Nicola—human. You struggle with the same flaws as the rest of the sheep, yet hold up your shield of virtue against all you consider imperfect. You spew your dogma regarding a righteousness you yourself do not possess!"

"That's ridiculous."

"But, true! And, I, my dear, Nicola, returned as *I* was created. As angel."

Anger pulsed through her temples. "Don't you *dare* call yourself angel! I know—"

"You think you know! But, you know nothing, girl! Fine! Crawl back into your battered body where all your lies are stored and I will be back for you in the morning!" He turned and spoke to someone behind him. "She's all yours."

Sight of the red demon shattered her resolve. "No!" All bravado vanished. Her body started to tremble. She shook her head back and forth. "No...no." Tyras was right. She was weak. She lifted her hand to beg him back. To accept his promises and comfort. But, he turned his back on her and left, slamming the door and leaving her to Poati.

Chapter 12

The Montero Estate

Black clouds hid the moon from sight, making the dark night darker. From the shadows of a small park, August leaned his shoulder against a tree and compared the number on the paper in his hand to the sign on the high, wrought-iron gate that surrounded the mansion across the street. *Pretty nice digs. And, well protected.*

Two burly guards stood just inside, behind bars with sharpened tips at the top, and spoke quietly to each other.

Kjin.

Easily detectable even from the distance that separated them.

So, not a wild goose chase after all. The mansion was clearly inhabited by demons.

August listened in on their conversation.

"Trust me, dude, we're better off out here. Have you seen Strand lately? The guy looks like he's eighty years old."

"I know. Maybe we should take off. Go somewhere else for a while."

"There's nowhere, man. He'd find us. Trust me."

August pushed away from the tree and headed straight for the gate. He could easily slip by the Kjin without detection if he wanted to, but he refused to pass up an opportunity to rid the world of two demons.

Tucking his fingertips into the front pocket of his jeans, he approached with a wide smile on his lips. "Evening, gentlemen."

The two Kjin turned and glared. Both were young. One thin with a goatee and the other more muscular with short, spiked hair.

Spike sneered. "No gentlemen here, kid. Keep moving."

"I'm hardly a kid. In fact, if my math is correct, let's see...sorry, it's been awhile...I was born fifty-eight years ago."

Goatee laughed and hit Spike on the arm. "Can you believe this guy?"

"Shut up!" Unlike Goatee, Spike understood. A machete materialized from behind his trench coat. "He's a Knight, idiot."

Goatee stepped back and eyed the lethal tips on the gate. "Think he can scale the gate?"

Spike shrugged. "I guess we'll see."

August also glanced up. "Yeah, I could do it, but that would be the hard way."

The two demons took another few steps back.

August shifted into wraith form, smiling at the surprised squeaks of the Kjin.

"Where did he go?"

"Let's get out of here!"

August shifted back, right behind Spike and stuck him in the back with his dagger. The Kjin released the breath in his lungs in an agonized grunt and disappeared in a flash of light. Goatee shrieked and took off at a sprint for the mansion. August was on him in seconds, bringing him to the ground. Another quick stab was all it took to end the demon's sordid existence in this world.

After a quick glance around, August ran toward the mansion at a crouch, hoping there were no surveillance cameras and, even if there were, that no one happened to be watching at the moment.

Somewhere nearby a dog barked. August went in the opposite direction, skirting the main entrance for the rear of the property.

Two more Kjin patrolled the grounds by a back entrance. *Why the heavy guard? An unusually paranoid Kjin leader or could it actually be Tyras hiding inside?* August's heart pounded at the thought that a brick wall may be all that separated him from the devil. But, first things first.

He whistled.

Both demons snapped their heads his way. He didn't shift this time as he wanted to draw the Kjin away from the door and all ears within screaming distance.

The over-confident guards rushed him together. The first to arrive pulled out a gun. "You lost buddy?"

"No, I'm looking for Tyras," he responded and struck the Kjin in the face with bone-breaking strength. The demon crumbled to the ground.

"You've got a set of balls, dude," the other Kjin said. "Coming here all by yourself for Tyras."

So, he is here.

August moved, hands blurring, lethal weapons that made quick work of ending the Kjin's life. He backed away as the guard fell to the ground and then stabbed both bodies with his dagger to make sure the shades within did not rise again. *Four down. How many more before I get to face Tyras himself. Five? Fifty?* Whatever it takes.

August ran to the back door and slammed the palm of his hand against the knob. The door popped open and he slipped into a large kitchen and shifted, unsure if the fight outside or the breaking door may have alerted anyone inside.

An invisible whisper of movement, he made his way through the kitchen and into a dimly lit hallway. Another Kjin in fatigues appeared and brushed by him. August followed the demon into a tiled foyer and watched him climb a grand staircase to an upper level.

Are you upstairs, Tyras? Time to introduce you to an Immortal weapon, devil.

August floated toward the stairs, but stopped when a tormented and decidedly female scream slashed the unnatural silence. It came from a lower level. *A human woman here with demons?* He growled inside his head. *I don't have time for this!* The scream came again. *Either does she.*

August sped back the way he came, searching for a way down. He finally found a door off the kitchen and shifted into physical form. He fled down winding stairs as far as they went and came out in a short hallway with a thick, arched door. The door opened at his touch, and he stepped into a dark corridor lined with cells, two on each side.

The smell of decay hit his senses hard and he had to swallow back the urge to be sick. He lifted his shirt and covered his nose, taking a few cautious steps forward. To his right, he saw the reason for the smell. An old woman lay dead, eyes open wide and unseeing. It looked as though she had been stabbed several times.

August continued forward slowly. To his left, one cell was empty, but another held a man, woman and small child huddled together in fright.

Soft moans came from the last cell on the right and something more sinister. A nauseating squelching sound.

August stopped and looked in, unable at first to process the scene before him. Red smears covered the entire cell floor. A girl lay motionless on the hard cement, her arms spread out to her sides, palms up. A small red demon hunched over her, nipping at her skin.

Shock and fury rolled over August in a wave. One well-placed kick at the cell door was all it took and he was in.

The demon whipped around to face him, red eyes glowing. August slammed his foot into the creature's temple sending him sliding into the wall with a high-pitched shriek.

The child across the hall started to scream and cry, but it was quickly muffled.

The demon stood, dazed, and shook his head. August advanced, pulling his dagger free. His first strike across the demon's abdomen did little damage, the hardened scales protecting the evil flesh beneath.

The demon tried to skitter away, but August caught his arm and held him fast. The creature hissed and screeched and snapped his teeth.

"Where is your Master?" August snarled out.

"Behind you."

August spun around and the demon leapt at him wrapping his arms and legs around his body. Realizing the ruse for what it was, August staggered back and crashed into the wall, pinning the wriggling demon between him and the concrete. "Don't want to talk, huh?" he taunted. "Then, enjoy your journey back to hell." August thrust his dagger over his shoulder and it hit true—directly in the little demon's eye. In a burst of white, the creature flashed out of the world.

August fell to his knees to catch his breath for just a moment before rushing to the girl and kneeling beside her. Fearing he might be too late, he felt for her pulse, but it was there steady and strong. He smoothed her blood-matted hair away from her face and gasped in horror. All the blood drained from his face and he rocked back on his heels. *No way! Nikki! How did she get here?*

He patted her chewed up cheeks. "Nikki, come on, baby, wake up."

"Is she all right?" said a little girl's voice, reminding August that he didn't have a lot of time.

Leaving Nikki, he ran to the cell holding the family. "Back up!" he ordered and as soon as they complied, kicked the door in. "Are you familiar with the house?" he asked the father. "There's a back door at the kitchen that's not guarded."

The man quickly gathered his family. "Yes, this is our house."

"Then, go. Run as fast as you can and don't look back."

"I don't plan to." But, the man did hesitate and he nodded in Nikki's direction. "Can you save her?"

August glanced over, hardly able to believe that the broken woman on the ground was Nikki. By some miracle, he had been given a second chance to do what he failed at all those years ago. "Yeah, I'm going to save her."

Tyras stood to walk around the desk when movement outside the window caught his eye. A man, woman and child were sprinting across the grounds to the gate. "Strand! They're escaping!" he roared, flipping the desk on its side.

"Who?"

"Our prisoners, you buffoon!" He strode toward the door. "How did they find me?"

"Who?" he asked again.

"The Knights of Emperica! Who else could it be?"

"Impossible!"

"Not impossible!" he retorted over his shoulder and crashed through the door of the study. He sprinted down the hallway, leaving the elderly Strand behind. "Someone is here to take my Nicola from me, Strand! Sadly for them, I will have to disappoint. And, it will not be painless, I can promise you that!"

Chapter 13

No Way Out

A voice called to Nikki from far away. *Tyras?* Did he come back to save her from Poati?

Strong arms urged her to get up. "Come on, Nikki, we're leaving."

She shook her head, the only part of her body still taking orders. "No...no, leave me. I...won't...marry you."

"Nikki!" Fingers on her chin turned her face. "It's me, babe."

"No. It...itches."

Hands rubbed her arms, bringing feeling back into her dead limbs. "Look at me."

She blinked her eyes to clear the haze and shrank back from the broad face and red eyes that hovered over her. "No," she groaned and turned her face.

"Look at me!"

Her will left her, leaving an empty shell behind. It felt like she had been fighting demons for a lifetime instead of five years, and she was done. She just wanted this over. She wanted to go home to happiness and peace. *It's too hard here. The fight never ends.*

"Look at me!"

Her eyes opened once again and the blunt face morphed into one she loved. *Ah, just another dream. August is here reaching for me again. If only it were true.*

"Hi, babe." His voice wrapped around her like a blanket. In that delicious moment, she decided to cling to the illusion for however long it lasted.

Dream August laughed out loud.

"You sound the same," she murmured.

"All right, enough, sleepy head. We're out of here."

Dream August lifted her into his arms, and that's when she noticed the tattoos on his arms. "Still have these, huh? They...make you look...tough. Just like your beard."

Lips pressed to her forehead. Gentle. Caring. She reached out to cup his cheek and his eyes caught hers. That's when she knew. It wasn't a dream. He was there with her in the flesh.

A grateful garbled mess came out of her mouth, but she didn't have the energy to decipher it. Apparently, neither did August.

"Shh, we'll talk when we get out of here, okay?"

His presence felt like a balm to her ruined body and weary mind. Strength flowed into her limbs and filled her with life. "I saw you on the news." It was a lame thing to say, but it's what came to mind.

"You did? I didn't know the devil was big on current affairs. Even if he is the cause of them."

"I can't believe you found me. I...I don't know how much longer I could have lasted. There was this demon, August, and he bit me and—"

"I know, he's dead," he said abruptly.

She had never been so happy to hear anything in her entire life. "Can you get us out of here, August?"

"Yes."

"Promise?"

"Yes." He angled her body to squeeze through the cell door. "Do you know if Tyras is here?"

The arched iron door slammed open revealing a furious Tyras. "Oh, yes, Knight, I am very much here."

Nikki's heart pounded out of control. Not for her, but for August. She already had her second chance at life and he deserved his. Darius sent him here for a reason, so he had to be pivotal in Emperica's plans. If anyone needed to be sacrificed in this fight, it was her. *If only I could fight!*

August put her down on the ground and calmly withdrew a dagger from his pocket that glowed similar to her Aventi.

Tyras stood at the end of the corridor, his nostrils flaring in anger, his thick arms bulging with barely restrained violence. Massive fingers clenched in and out of balled fists.

Nikki used the cell bars to haul herself to her feet behind August. She placed her hands on his hips in a sign of her support.

"Nicola, step back!" Tyras bellowed.

"You expect her to lie down and not fight for her life?" August asked.

"I do not wish to end her life. Just yours."

"She would rather be dead in Emperica than alive with you."

Tyras' lip curled with rage. August hit a nerve. The devil really believed that he would have her in his life. Really thought she could eventually accept him. A delusion based on his narcissism. And, her ruse, she readily admitted. Her stalling led him to think along those lines.

Only now it was August who was going to pay the price for that deception.

∽

August bladed his body to fight in the small hallway with Nikki pressing her hands into his back. She had no weapon, but by Tyras' own admission, he didn't wish to harm her so that could work for them.

August took a good look at the adversary he hadn't seen in an age. He wasn't sure what he had expected, but this beefy giant wasn't it. He looked like he could crack August's skull in one hand. August twirled his dagger and twitched a shoulder.

Time to find out.

He curled his fingers in a taunting gesture and Tyras came at him in a ball of muscled ferocity. He braced himself for the physical collision, but grunted in surprise when Tyras shot out a hand and he was lifted off his feet and slammed against the wall. His dagger fell from his hand as something hard pressed against his throat, cutting off his airway. Pinned by an otherworldly force he couldn't fight, August struggled to breathe against the burning pressure in his lungs.

Twenty feet away, Tyras' clawed hand squeezed stealing the life from him. He kicked his heels into the cement wall and bucked against the power that held him.

"August!" Nikki screamed and rushed to his side, although there was nothing she could do. She charged toward Tyras. "Leave him alone!"

"And, what will you give me if I let him live, Nicola?"

"You're killing him! Let him go!"

Tyras' red eyes burned with desire. "What, Nicola?"

She dropped to her knees. "Let him go."

"And...?"

"Don't make me say it," she whispered.

"You will be my wife! There, I said it for you! It's really not that difficult, Nicola."

With a flick of Tyras' wrist, August fell to the ground and clutched his neck, sucking in a life-saving breath of air.

Tyras stalked forward, grabbed Nikki's arm and lifted her to her feet. "Get back in the cell," he ordered, and she meekly complied. August wanted to tell her not to do it, but he couldn't get enough breath through his constricted windpipe. Tyras kicked Nikki's cell door shut and locked it. "I won't kill him," he told her. "But, he must pay for what he did. He tried to take you from me and he must learn the futility of rebellion. And, you, my dear, will watch."

Tyras turned to August with his arms crossed at his chest. "Pick up your weapon."

August hesitated at first, unsure what kind of game the devil played. Surely, he would prefer August to be unarmed. It wasn't as though he had any honorable intentions in that regard. Cautiously, August picked up his dagger and got to his feet. The moment he armed himself, Tyras closed the distance between them faster than August thought possible for a man of his size. A meaty hand lashed out and backhanded him across the cheek.

August's head whipped to the side followed by a string of blood that splattered across the floor. He caught Tyras' second strike on his forearm, barely deflecting the strength of the shot. In return, he hammered a fist forward and pain ricocheted through his entire arm upon contact with Tyras' stone face.

"Is that all you have, rodent?" Tyras sneered.

Damn it! August leapt toward the cell door on the right, took two running steps up the side and pushed off, twisting in the air. He drove his dagger downward, aiming for Tyras' neck, snarling with his need to feel the bite of flesh beneath his hand. But, the Emperical weapon slid harmlessly away from Tyras without leaving a single scratch. As a result, August slammed to the floor with a groan.

"August!" Nikki screamed.

Tyras issued a booming laugh. "You would leave me for this?" he asked Nikki. "He's worthless!"

Tyras bent over August, picked him up by the scruff of his neck as though he weighed no more than a child and threw him into the wall.

"Leave him alone!"

Ignoring Nikki's pleas, he pummeled August with both fists. August tried to get out from under the hulking giant, but Tyras was just too big. Too strong. Too intractable.

Mercifully, August's vision started to fade and he felt himself drift away toward unconsciousness away from the pain. But, not before he felt Tyras grab his legs and haul him into the cell across from Nikki's.

Through eyes already starting to swell shut, August watched Tyras stalk to Nikki's cell. "You have an hour to give me your answer, Nicola. As much as I enjoy your company, I will kill you if you do not commit yourself to me. Of your own free will."

The thud of Tyras' retreating boot steps echoed in the small chamber.

Before darkness swallowed August completely, one fact rose above the others in his mind. Their new weapons didn't work on Tyras.

He was undefeatable.

Chapter 14

Answered Prayers

Nikki scratched furiously at the wounds on her legs and arms, the itch unbearable as the skin started to weave back together. She didn't know how much time had passed since Tyras made his threat, but knew it had to be close to an hour. When he came back, she would have to decide between death for herself and August or a life of sin at the devil's side. *As if there had ever been a choice.* If August could talk, he would agree with her. He stopped moaning a while ago so he may even be dead already.

She tried not to look at Dr. Morris' rotting corpse, but every breath she took reminded her of its existence. She envied the doctor already in Emperica and envisioned her standing before the gates and the Paties rushing out to greet her. As happy as she was for Dr. Morris, it brought sadness to her heart to think of what her family would have to go through at her disappearance.

Frustration surged through her. Unable to do anything but sulk and wait for Tyras, she slammed her elbow into the wall behind her and it made a loud thunk.

"Settle down, Knight. How much time do we have?"

Nikki's hand flew to her mouth. *August!* She scrambled to her feet and ran to the bars of the cell surprised to see him standing up. "You're okay?"

A frown creased his forehead. "Why wouldn't I be? My injuries, although painful, were superficial. We do heal, you know, Nikki."

"I know, but I haven't been able to heal quickly in Tyras' presence. I guess you haven't been here long enough to have it affect you yet." She grabbed the bars and jerked them back and forth in desperation. "He's going to be here any minute, August! And, I just..."

"Just, what?"

She shook her head. "I...I know it sounds stupid, but I just wish I could...I don't know...touch you one last time before he comes. It won't be the same when we get back to Emperica!"

A sweet smile lightened his face. "So, you missed me?"

"Yes, I missed you. A lot."

"It's weird."

Humiliation colored her cheeks. "Weird?"

He scratched the stubble on his jaw. "I've just been beaten to a bloody pulp. You've been tortured for days. In moments, we'll be fleeing for our lives from the most dangerous being walking this earth and all I want to do is kiss you."

Her breathing hitched in her chest and she bit her lip to keep from crying. "Hard to do with a wall of steel between us."

"Not hard for me."

"What—?" The room lit up in a nimbus of light. Nikki stumbled back in shock when August shifted into wraith form. Her heart thudded with unbelievable joy at sight of the glowing form, the epitome of all that was beautiful and pure. The embodiment of home.

August slid easily through the bars of his cell and crossed to hers. He reached inside and cupped her face and it felt like the tickle of a warm summer breeze. She closed her eyes and basked in his touch, in his love.

And, then it was gone.

He shifted back into physical form. "Stand back."

She did as he asked and he kicked in the door to her cell, something she had been unable to do. Whatever new powers he brought with him from Emperica were far superior to hers.

He reached in and grabbed her hand. "Run now, talk later."

"Wait! The Monteros!"

"Gone."

She yelped when he pulled her forcefully from the cell and sprinted out of the dungeon. As they rushed up the stairs, Nikki prayed that Tyras wouldn't find them, but she realized how small the chances of that miracle. The devil wouldn't let her leave easily. With a hand on August's back, she pushed him ahead, dreading the inevitable, bracing herself for Tyras' hulking form to appear out of nowhere and block their path.

They crashed through the cellar door just as an ungodly roar came from the upper level. Her frazzled nerves dropped her to her knees and her hands came up to cover her ears. But, August wouldn't let her waver. He grabbed her elbow and yanked her back to her feet. "Move it, Knight!" he yelled, and she stumbled behind after him once again.

We need a miracle!

"This way!" She took the lead and sprinted through the living room to the foyer. She skidded to a stop when she saw a body lying on the floor next to the front door. Despite the advanced age of the dead Kjin, she recognized the short hair and fatigues. "Looks like his age caught up with him," she commented to herself.

"Who is he?" August asked.

"Our miracle."

She kissed two fingers and raised them upward as they escaped out the door and into the night.

Tyras stood with his back to the Kjin and his hands clasped tightly behind him. "Repeat what you just said."

The demon hesitated. "The Knights are gone, Master. Both of them."

The fire of wrath awakened in Tyras' body leaving a trail of red, molten fury in its wake. He was transported back in time. Back to his first days in Mordeaux when the fire had been born within him. When he first learned to control the elemental power to which he was now intricately bound. At one point, the sentient spirit sought to destroy him. The battle of wills lasted for days, but Tyras stubbornly held on until he wrestled the age-old entity back into submission.

Now, though, the fire fared to life again in a challenge for dominance. Maybe due to the unadulterated anger coursing through him. More likely, it was simply an opportunist moment, the fire sensing him in a vulnerable state.

Whatever the reason, the power struggle ignited anew. Flames burst to life and danced over his skin. Heat scoured the marrow of his bones and boiled the blood in his veins. Tyras snarled, grasping the window sill in front of him, batting back the blistering burn. His body trembled. He fell to one knee. Minutes passed as he fought to douse the blaze before it could take hold.

It worked.

The fire inside finally retreated and was his to command once again.

Tyras stood, clenched his fists and bellowed his victory at the top of his lungs. The flower vase burst into a shower of crystal and dead, crumpled leaves. The picture window exploded in shards of glass. Whirling on the Kjin at the door, Tyras threw out a hand and sent a ball of fire directly at his chest. The demon screamed and ran, but Tyras knew he wouldn't get far. The fire would see to that.

Tyras stalked from the study, throwing fire as he went. *Let it burn! Let it all burn!* He passed the engulfed demon writhing on the floor and thundered down the stairs. There, at the bottom, he found proof of Nicola's betrayal. Strand's dead body in front of the open door. Poati must have met a similar fate otherwise he would be here.

He was alone now.

Black smoke poured from the upper level. An old woman staggered down the stairs with a cloth over her nose and mouth.

No, not quite alone. "Stella! Stella, come here at once!"

The woman almost tripped down the last few steps when she saw the body on the ground. "We must leave, Mr. Smith!"

"I hope you know how to drive, woman."

"What? Yes...yes, of course."

"Come," he said, propelling her forward by the elbow. "You are taking me to Tennessee."

"Tennessee? I...I'm not sure..."

Tyras pushed her toward the door. "Get moving."

Stella nodded and led the way around the house, presumably to where the vehicles were kept. She turned back once and surprise colored her expression. "Mr. Smith! Your shoes are burning!"

Tyras nodded. "Yes, they are," he confirmed, ignoring the trail of burnt rage left in his wake.

CHAPTER 15

Impossible Dreams

Battle raged all around her. Vile chants filled the air. An insistent, powerful wind tugged at her, dragging her closer to death. Blane swung his Aventi at the demons who tried to corral the Knights into that dangerous eddy.

"It's not working!" he yelled.

Nikki turned to him, her hair whipping furiously around her head.

No, it wasn't Blane. It was August who spoke.

But, August wasn't at Baylor's Pass.

She had no time to analyze further. Her feet swept out from under her. August grabbed her arms just in time and held on. Tears stained his face as he tried to wrench her from the pull of the deadly vortex.

"Let me go!" she begged. "Save yourself!"

"It's too late," his lips mouthed mournfully. And, together, they were sucked into the demon-made portal. White hot agony lanced through her as a thousand knives entered her body and her mind was shredded into tiny pieces.

Nikki awoke screaming.

An arm quickly pulled her close. "Relax. You're okay. I've got you."

Her first instinct to fight brought her fist up toward her assailant's head, but he caught her arm in a steel grip. "Nikki! You're fine. It's me."

She let out a heavy breath when she recognized the voice and slumped back into the car seat. "Sorry, I just had the strangest dream."

"Want to talk about it?" August asked.

She shook her head. "No, not really."

"Okay."

She ran a hand through her tangled hair remembering their harrowing escape into the rainy night. "Where are we?"

He shrugged. "Not sure exactly. But, I know we're pointed in the right direction." He patted the GPS unit on top of the dash. "You programmed our route before you fell asleep. I just pulled over at a rest stop to get a few hours of sleep myself."

"Good idea."

A curtain of rain pelted the car outside, isolating them. Nikki couldn't see anything beyond their little dark world lit only by the dim light of the dash. It felt both eerie and comforting. Had she really escaped Tyras' prison? Or, like so many times before, would the blink of an eye find her back on the concrete floor of her cell.

It took several minutes and a few bats of her eyelids to convince herself that she actually was safe—at least for the moment. The nightmare Tyras represented still existed, but at least now she could go out fighting with the Order and not at the devil's hand. All thanks to August. *How did he find me?* She glanced over to find him staring at her with an intensity that surprised her. Something primal inside her shifted at that look.

"I'm glad we're back together," he told her.

"Me, too." She rubbed the goose bumps from her arms.

"You cold?"

"Just tired of being wet."

"Do you want my shirt?"

She smiled. "No, I'll be fine." Suddenly feeling self-conscious, she raised a hand to her cheek. "How does my face look?"

"Perfect."

She slapped his arm and pulled down the mirror on the visor to check. *Thank goodness.* All of the pits had healed completely.

"Should we get going?" he asked.

The suggestion brought a stab of panic to her heart. This might be the last time they would ever have alone together in human form. She turned in the seat to look at him and a lump formed in her throat. *He came for me.* Somehow, some way, he came. Gratitude turned to desire. She reached for his hand wanting so badly for him to kiss her right then. To feel the strength of his lips on hers and to help her forget—just for a moment—the endless fight that took everything from them. *Is it selfish to ask for a brief reprieve?*

August must have read her mind. He leaned over and pulled her close bringing his mouth down on hers. Their tongues met in an erotic tangle of pure pleasure. Someone moaned. It could have been either one of them for all her mind could process a coherent thought.

Her body ached with need. The connection between them so pure, so raw, that it sent a harsh throb of longing through her. In August's arms, the devil had no place. She clung to him, drinking in the taste of him. Reveling in the feel of his hard muscles beneath her hands.

Abruptly, he pulled back. "I...I can't."

"What?" she asked in a breathless whisper, embarrassed at how caught up she had been in a simple kiss. "What's the matter?"

"It's hard to explain."

If he doesn't want me, I'd rather know now. Nikki reached over and brushed her fingers over the blonde scruff on his chin. "Try. I can take it. I promise."

"We can't be together.

"Ouch." Nikki's hand fell away from his face. "A crowbar would have been kinder."

"You don't understand."

She snorted. "No, I guess I don't."

He slammed his palm on the steering wheel. "I'm an Immortal, Nikki!"

Her mouth fell open in shock. "An Immortal? How did that happen?"

"I've always been an Immortal."

"You're not making any sense, August. What are you talking about?"

He swallowed. "I'm not who you think I am."

"Look, if you don't want to be with me—"

"Nikki! I am Antonius! One of the original twelve angels created at the beginning of time. I fought in the Holy War that sent Tyras to exile and I've been fighting this war against the Kjin ever since."

She shook her head. "Uh...no. You're August Rand. The boy who grew up down the street from me. You like fast cars and tattoos and we graduated from the same high school."

"That's not me."

"Of course it's you! We died together in a car accident. You're telling me what we had wasn't real?"

It was real to me. I've loved you forever. You just don't remember. "There's a lot I just can't get into right now."

"Oh, no, you don't. You can't just make crazy claims like that and blow me off. I need to know what's going on, August."

"You will, I promise. Just not right now, okay?"

A long silence, broken only by the occasional frustrated sigh by Nikki, filled the car. Finally, she turned back to him. "You're really Antonius?"

"Yes."

"But, Tyras is one of the original twelve, too. Why didn't he recognize you?"

"I look quite a bit different than when we knew each other last. As does he. A few millennia will do that to you."

Another silence. Shorter this time.

"So, why can't we be together?"

"Isn't it obvious? I'm Immortal and you're human."

"That's a stupid reason. After all we've been through? All we still face?"

He turned and stared out into the rain. "I love you, Nikki, more than you know, but I forgot until just this moment how much it hurts. I can't love you again just to lose you in a few years."

Didn't she realize that the peace of Emperica was no longer an option for him? When she was gone, he would be stuck down here haunted by her loss for an eternity. Even now after only a few hours together, the thought of letting her go burned a hole in his stomach the size of a rock. An eternity wasn't long enough to make him ever forget her scent, the curve of her jaw, her big brown eyes. What they shared together was powerful. So much more than the childhood fling she believed it to be.

"We better go," he said abruptly and started the car.

"Okay, but promise me one thing."

"What?"

"Just don't give up on me yet," she whispered.

CHAPTER 16

Too Close to Home

"Your foot is pressing into my ribcage," Fallon grumbled.

Blane snorted. "Well, your elbow is about to make me sterile."

"Oh, is *that* what that is? I thought it was a—"

"Be careful!"

Fallon shook her head and moved her elbow. From her perch thirty feet in the air, she could see that the soldier below was still being held at gunpoint. Another hour up here and she might just kill Brad Murphy herself.

Light coming from the high windows that lined two sides of the building, told her it was now dawn. The activity in the training center increased as more soldiers came and went, hurrying about their business. Some were Kjin, some human. Murphy had lied about the soldiers being held hostage and by their conversations during the night, it was clear that they had no idea that demons walked among them. They just assumed they were following the orders of General Nash. Although, a few did complain that it didn't seem to be protocol to keep one of their own at gunpoint and civilian prisoners dangling in a net above their heads. Even if said prisoners were *terrorists*.

That didn't sit well with Blane. "Oh, they call us terrorists when they're working for the freaking devil!" he hissed at one point.

Another cramp rippled through Fallon's calf muscle, but she couldn't reach her leg to rub it out. They had to do something soon. But, what?

"So, what are we going to do?" Joseph asked.

Fallon wasn't surprised the Immortal's thoughts echoed her own. He didn't say much, but when he did it was usually to prompt Blane into action.

"Why don't you shift and go down there and use some demons as target practice with that bow of yours?" Blane suggested.

"For the same reason we don't cut ourselves free now. If I start killing, they start killing. The first on their list would be the poor soldier that led us here."

Blane glared down at Brad Murphy. "That *poor* soldier tricked us!"

"I doubt he had much say in the matter," Fallon said. "And, Joseph is right. We can't jeopardize the lives of all of the other innocents down there."

The sound of a door opening had Fallon twisting around to try and get a look, but all she got was an elbow from Blane for it. Still, in her peripheral vision, she could see a large door opening in the side of the training center. Soldiers scattered out of the way as a military jeep rumbled inside. When it stopped, a man in a suit and opened necked white shirt stepped out.

"Billingsley," Blane whispered. He obviously had a much better view than she did.

"What's he doing?"

"Looking at us. Pointing...oh, now that's not nice. He just flipped us off."

"Is he Kjin?"

"Yeah."

They had suspected for a long time that Governor Billingsley and General Nash were Kjin, but it was still disheartening to finally get the proof. Men in high-level positions like that could destroy the world even without Tyras' help. She only hoped the Immortal Vincent had been able to get the President underground.

"He's moving now toward a back room," Blane advised. "Probably to plot our demise."

The sound of muted vibration cut through their conversation.

"What is that?" Joseph asked.

Fallon wiggled her body to get to her pocket. "My phone. Someone's texting me."

"You're going to read a text? Now?" Blane asked incredulously.

She lifted her shoulders. "Why not? It's not like I'm *tied up* or anything."

"Cute."

She read the text. "Uh, oh."

"What?"

"Time to cut loose."

"Why?"

"That was Kade. He asked me what I wanted for breakfast."

"I don't get it."

"If he's asking me that, it can only mean—"

A loud revving engine and screeching tires drowned out her words. And, it was getting closer. "Hang on." As soon as the words left her mouth, a green military jeep crashed through the closing door and careened into the vehicle used to transport the governor. The driver backed up to shake loose of the other jeep's bumper and Juliet stuck her head out the window and waved.

"What is she doing? Hurry! Get us down!" Blane screamed, but Fallon had already cut through the net, releasing the three of them into midair.

Kade spun around the center recklessly sending soldiers diving for cover. At least it kept them distracted from shooting which was probably why he was doing it.

Fallon hit the ground smoothly and waited for the jeep.

Kade finally got the vehicle pointed toward the exit and hit the accelerator. He slowed only for a second to allow them an opportunity to dive into the open-sided vehicle. When they were all in, Fallon hit the back of Kade's seat. "Go!"

She watched Blane reach over the front, grab Juliet's face, and kiss her. "You're in big trouble."

Juliet chuckled.

That girl really didn't take things seriously enough, Fallon thought with a shake of her head. Blane needed to have a talk with her. Soon.

And, then all thoughts of Juliet vanished as Kade peeled out of the training center, tires smoking.

The sharp retort of gunfire followed their vehicle.

"Get down!"

Kade tore off across the tarmac and headed toward the bunker. Bullets ripped through the rear canvas.

"Son of a bitch!" Juliet swore.

"We have a child in the car, potty mouth," Blane admonished her.

Blane's dark-haired wife twisted around. "We do?"

"Yeah, Joseph, meet my wife, Juliet. Juliet, Joseph."

Juliet gave him a rueful smile. "Oh, hey, sorry, kid."

Joseph just smiled in that odd way of his. Then, he turned to Fallon. "I'm going back. Now, that you're safe I'll go take care of Billingsley."

A sudden protectiveness reared inside her. "No, let me go. I'll find a uniform to wear. Because of my height, I can blend in better than you can."

He smiled. "I can disappear, Fallon."

She smiled back feeling like a fool, but couldn't help but think of him as a child. "It will still be dangerous. Let me do it."

"That's why I'm here, Fallon. To save lives." He reached out and put a small hand on her belly. "Your son's life as well."

She sucked in a surprised breath, but the Immortal simply gave her a wink and disappeared from view.

"Where did he go?" Blane asked, but Fallon ignored him.

A son? A guess or something more? She remembered the child from the train wreck that Joseph healed. Just as Blane had powers she didn't possess, the Immortal seemed to have his own arsenal to draw from. A knot formed in her throat as she caressed the tiny bulge of her belly. It felt right. Now convinced that the baby inside her was a boy, new emotions bubbled to the surface and threatened to spill over. It was all she could do to stop herself from bawling. *Kade's son. My son. Whatever it takes, I will protect you, little guy, I promise.*

With a great deal of effort, she wrangled her feelings under control. Soon, she would allow herself time to shed happy tears, but not now. Not with Tyras wandering free. Although they still had no idea where he was, she had a feeling that for better or worse, they would soon find out. She glanced back through the rear opening and hissed in shock. "A Black Knight!"

"Got it!" Kade answered and stepped on the pedal.

"He's gaining on us!" Blane yelled.

The Black Knight tore after them, running as fast as an angel despite the heavy black armor he wore.

"Ready your weapons!" she warned. Mere seconds later, the heavy canvas roof bulged downward. "He's on the roof!" Fallon watched in horror as a black, gauntleted hand reached in through the driver's side and grabbed Kade by his leather jacket. The Knight grunted in effort and yanked Kade bodily out of the jeep. The car veered to the left and Juliet screamed and reached for the steering wheel.

Fallon didn't hesitate. She did what any warrior wife would do. She jumped out of the moving vehicle after her husband.

༄

After Fallon jumped out of the jeep, Blane crawled into the front seat and slammed on the brakes, sending the vehicle fishtailing across the rain-slicked blacktop. With one hand loosely holding the steering wheel, his other shot out across Juliet's chest and pinned her to the seat. When the jeep rocked to a violent stop, he pulled her shaking body close. "Stay here, Juliet and I mean it. If you can't do it for me, do it for Teddy and Georgie."

"But—"

"You don't understand! *I* can't even defeat this Black Knight. We're going to have to depend on Joseph to do it. Please, honey, just stay here."

She didn't respond, but he had no time to spend arguing. He would just have to protect her if she did anything stupid. With a frustrated growl, he got out of the car and sprinted toward Fallon and Kade. Fallon seemed to be having the same discussion with Kade, but he wasn't having any of it. Blood dripped from his face, but he had somehow managed to find a metal rod that he hefted back and forth in his hands, apparently gauging its damage potential.

"Where's Joseph?" Blane screamed, skidding to a stop.

"He's gone," Fallon told him.

"Where? We need an Immortal for this!"

Fallon lifted her shoulders. "He went back to go after Billingsley. I couldn't stop him."

"Great." Blane eyed Kade's rod. "And, what are you going to do with that?"

"Ram it through its eye if I can. Most brains can't withstand that kind of thing." Kade paused. "It does have a brain, doesn't it?"

Blane shook his head. "All right. Let's do this." He turned to face the Knight, took a deep breath and started forward slowly, Fallon and Kade flanking him. The Mordeaux demon stood immobile, watching them come. Toying with them Blane knew because at any moment, the demon could unleash that black lightning and vaporize them. "If we can get past his shield and armor, our Aventis might work," Blane told Fallon.

"We'll never get that close," she said, sounding worried. He watched her hand once again drift to her stomach.

"It's all we have. I'll go directly at him. You and Kade circle around."

Without waiting for a response, Blane launched himself forward activating his Aventi as he went, although he had no intention of using it. His fight at the train wreck proved the futility of that strategy. No, he had to get the Knight on the ground somehow. If he did that, it might just give Kade the opportunity he needed to use that metal rod of his.

Blane stumbled to a stop when the Black Knight pointed his sword toward the ground and once again called forth help from the underworld. A black, crackling line of electricity jumped from the ground to the tip of the sword. The Knight laughed as the energy filled him—a brutal, sick sound.

"Hey, ugly! Over here!" Juliet stood behind the Knight waving her arms.

Time stood still and Blane could hardly breathe. His lungs shriveled, devoid of all air. His heart stopped beating.

"I'm over here, stupid!" she shouted again.

The Black Knight spun and swept his sword outward, releasing a rope of black death directly at her.

"No!" Blane dropped to his knees in terror. He wanted to look away, didn't want to remember the day his life ended, but he knelt wide-eyed and riveted to the scene before him. The lightning streaked forward while Juliet just stood there waiting to die. She didn't fall to the ground or try to run. *She's sacrificing herself for me! Just like she tried to do at Baylor's Pass!*

Their short life together flashed through his mind. The first time he saw her waitressing at The Blackstone. Onstage smiling and singing her sad songs. Rocking Teddy or Georgie to sleep. Making love to him, her eyes lidded and face flushed.

He never felt more alive than when he was in her arms. He was supposed to be the one that protected her, but Juliet knew the truth. In the dark of the night, it was she who comforted him. She who calmed his fears and made him feel wanted and loved.

Please, he prayed. *I can't lose her.*

Suddenly, a dazzling beam of light rocketed through the air and intercepted the Knight's lightning. The twin powers clashed in an eruption of sparks, the might of Mordeaux and Emperica pitted together through the weapons of their champions.

Joseph? Blane followed the light. *No, Vincent!*

The Immortal growled and ran at the Black Knight, shortening the link between them. A quick twist of his wrist wound the lasso of light and the black lightning around the demon pinning his arms to his side. The Knight screamed as his sword fell from his hand, severing the connection to Mordeaux.

Fallon flew at the demon from the right and kicked with both feet, sending him crashing to the ground in a lumbering fall. Kade finally put that rod to use by using it to pry open the Knight's helm and driving the blunt end into its eye.

Vincent ended it all by unwinding the lasso and flicking it back toward the body, sending both shade and corpse back to where they came from.

Blane hung his head in overwhelming relief. He was still on his knees when Juliet approached. She didn't say anything. She simply wrapped her arms around his head and pressed him close. He clung to her. In his mind, he had already lost her and it would take a moment to convince his galloping heart that she was still here with him.

"I'm sorry," she whispered after a time. "I won't put you through that again."

He nodded, grateful that she finally understood what it did to him. He stood and took her in his arms. They stayed together for long moments, neither of them ready or able to break apart.

Finally, he sent a cautious look back toward the training center, but the soldiers were nowhere in sight. "Come on," he said, draping an arm around Juliet's shoulder and walking her over to where the others stood waiting for them.

The gray-haired Immortal clapped Blane on the back as soon as they approached. "Good to see you again, Knight. Hope you don't mind that I used your wife. I needed a distraction."

His lips pressed into a thin line. "Actually, I do mind. Don't do it again."

"She was never really in any danger—"

"Never. Again."

Juliet smiled at Vincent. "He's kind of possessive."
"Yeah, I'm getting that."

CHAPTER 17

Back from the Dead

Fallon's fingers accidently brushed the knot on Kade's head and he winced.

"Sorry."

He didn't open his eyes, just made a content, murmuring sound as he lay back against her with his head in her lap. Holding an umbrella with one hand, she continued to smooth his hair—which was still too long—back behind one ear. She yawned, wishing she could join him and just sleep for a few hours, but that was unlikely to happen for some time now.

After the confrontation with the Black Knight, they had all wondered why the soldiers at the training center didn't give chase—until they saw the entire Reglan team of angels lined up atop the bunker. Turns out Kade and Juliet didn't come alone. *Good.* Now, that they knew where the Kjin were gathering, they would make their stand here.

The Knights, now huddled under the wooden structure, were busy handing out food, but she convinced Kade to go further down the wall for some privacy.

A smile pulled up the corners of her mouth as she looked down at him. She loved him so much. From the very first day they met, they had been drawn together. He to her because of his Intuit tendencies and she to him because of his kindness and bravery. Not too many men who heard her story would have stuck around for long. But, Kade had. Partially due to an attraction so potent, so...extraordinary that neither one of them ever had a chance.

Even when she tried to erase his memory.

The paranormal connection that linked them also protected his mind, and she was grateful beyond words that it hadn't worked.

She debated telling him about the baby. On one hand, this child was his just as much as hers and he deserved to know. But on the other, the knowledge would make him more reckless in his attempts to try and protect her. *More reckless than usual anyway.*

He must have sensed her unease. "What's wrong?"

She smiled. "Just thinking that you really should stop jumping out of moving vehicles."

"Er, I had a little help on that one." He reached up and cupped her face, rubbing his thumb across her cheek. "But, my angel has to stop following me into the fire."

She tried to swallow past the stinging burn in her throat. "I'd follow you anywhere to get you back."

"You're never afraid, are you?" he asked with a trace of awe in his voice.

"I'm afraid of waking up without you."

He sat up to look at her. The dimples deepened. The love in his eyes shone. So bright that it brought tears to her eyes. Now, was the perfect time to tell him what their love had created. A piece of him and a piece of her.

"Kade...there's something I need to—"

"Fallon! Kade!"

Her words cut off at the appearance of Blane, Juliet and Vincent.

"Hold that thought," Kade told her and turned to the trio. "Any luck reaching August?" he asked them, completely oblivious to the fact that she was just about to change his life forever.

Vincent shook his head. "No, he doesn't answer his cell."

"That means I'm taking over again," Blane declared. "If Joseph is able to deal with Billingsley, we may be able to reason with the soldiers inside and get them to lay down their arms. If not, we'll have to go in."

Juliet jumped up on the stone wall to look over their heads. "Then, you're going to need a lot more Knights."

Fallon scrambled up to see what she was taking about. A line of jeeps and soldiers on foot lined the western horizon. Hundreds. And, how many of them were Kjin, they had no way of knowing just yet. *We're in trouble here. Even without the devil.*

Kade asked the question on all their minds. "Do you think Tyras is in the group?"

Vincent cracked his knuckles. "If he is, you leave him to me."

"All I know is, we're severely outnumbered now. Wait! Who is that?" Blane asked, pointing to the east.

Fallon turned and squinted into the gloom. Two people ran toward them at a supernatural pace. Angels for sure. Then, she noticed the leather vest. "It's August!" She felt profound relief at having all of the Immortals back with them.

"You've got to be shittin' me."

"Juliet!" Blane scolded his wife.

"Don't you see who that is with him?" she asked, ignoring his reprimand.

Blane stepped up beside Fallon to get a closer look. She felt him stiffen beside her at the same time she recognized the flowing auburn hair and easy gait. *Nikki.* Against all odds, she made it back to them.

Blane pumped his fist in the air and raced off to greet their friend.

Fallon smiled, suddenly not feeling so outnumbered. And, it wasn't just the unexpected appearance of another Immortal. It was Nikki. There was something unique about her. A fierce warrior for sure, but also an old soul. An anchor in the storm. Someone who could comfort with the smallest look or touch.

Despite the rain, Fallon felt like the world just got a little bit brighter.

⌘

Nikki's gaze kept sliding to the east. She had hoped to see sun again after escaping Tyras' clutches, but found only the same dreary skies that chased her and August across three states. And, it was getting worse, making it hard to ignore the obvious. Tyras was coming closer. He wasn't here yet, but he was coming.

She walked with Blane and Fallon down the long row of Knights. Here and there, soft conversation took place, but most stood quiet, waiting for an order.

Blane put his arm around Nikki and gave her a squeeze. "I've missed you."

"Yeah, you already said that, boss. A few times now."

Fallon chuckled and put her arm around Nikki's waist as well. "I'm glad you're back, too. You're the only one who can make this old curmudgeon smile," she said with a nod toward Blane.

"Curmudgeon?" Blane scoffed. "No one says that today, Fallon."

"Well, we aren't of today, are we?"

"No, my wife reminds me how socially inept I am all the time. Claims that's why she keeps me locked in the bedroom," he said with a wiggle of his eyebrows.

"Bragger."

He laughed and steered them away from the bunker and out into the rain. Nikki sighed. It seemed she was destined to be perpetually wet.

"So, tell us what happened, Nikki," Blane said. "I have to know before I commit the Order to this fight. What happened after you went through the portal?"

She took a deep breath, really not wanting to go back there...to the weeks with Tyras, but knew she had to. "I don't remember going through the portal at all. When I awoke, I was in an unfamiliar bedroom being looked after by a private doctor." An image of Dr. Morris' rotting corpse floated across her mind, but she pushed it aside.

"Did you see him?"

"Tyras? Yes, he's here." Low murmurs of discontent filtered through the group. "He admitted to dragging me from Mordeaux initially to use as a pawn, but then to take...well, to take as his wife."

"His wife?" Blane exploded. "As if a Knight of Emperica would ever turn against the light! He's delusional."

Nikki didn't bring up the fact that Justus had in fact done that very thing. She also didn't agree that Tyras was delusional. She had time to replay many of their conversations in her mind and everything pointed to him being quite sane. Calculating, but reasoned. Ambitious yet cautious. Tyras knew exactly what he wanted and evaluated the steps necessary to achieve his goals before committing resources. That's what made him so dangerous.

"It would help if we destroy this nest of Kjin *before* he arrives. Tyras is not as delusional as you think, but he will not spare the innocent to get what he wants."

"And, what does he want?"

"The world."

A thoughtful silence settled between them as they walked.

"I'm sorry you had to go through that," Fallon finally said. "But, you're safe now. As safe as a warrior can get anyway."

"The problem is going to be ferreting out the demons from the humans," Blane said, getting back to the point. "This battle is going to get ugly and innocent people will be trying to kill us."

"And, driven by patriotic honor. They think we're here to harm Americans."

"I'm going to send the Immortals in first," Blane said. "Between the three of them, they can take out a good number of Kjin and while they provide their diversion, we can go in after the leaders. Even if...*when*...Tyras appears, the human soldiers will be less likely to take orders from him without their chain of command intact."

Nikki flinched when two muscular arms encircled her waist. Immediately, a sense of security and warmth flowed through her.

August.

"So, you're sending the Immortals in, right?" he asked Blane over her shoulder.

Blane nodded. "Do you have a problem with that?"

"No, it makes sense. It's what I would have done." Nikki yelped when he spun her around and cradled her face in his hands. "And, so does this." His pressed his lips to hers and said for her ears alone, "Only sometimes you don't know how much until you let her go."

"Does that mean...?"

"It means none of *this*," he said waving his hand, "makes sense without you. None of the sacrifice has value if you shun the thing you're trying to protect."

"But...it doesn't change the fact that when I die, we'll never see each other again. Ever."

"It's a pain I'm willing to endure to have you now."

"Why? What changed your mind?"

"Joseph."

"Joseph? Did he come back?"

"Yeah, he's right behind me." August turned around to prove his point, but no one was there. "Well, he was right behind me." He shrugged and pulled Nikki to the side for privacy. "Trust me, I just talked to him a few minutes ago. That kid's pretty smart. I think he has visions or something. Anyway, he told me that my logic is flawed. Love is not conditional. It's a gift. You don't love someone only if you can have them for a certain number of years. You love them because you can't live without them. For whatever time you have. And, even though that's about the corniest thing that has ever come out of my mouth, I mean every single word."

She jumped in his arms and kissed his forehead. "Do you mean it?" He nodded so she kissed each of his eyes. "Are you sure?" At his second nod, she kissed his nose. "You'll have to tell me quite a few times before I'm convinced." He growled out something unintelligible while she trailed her lips down his cheek to his mouth. "Just come back to me," she murmured.

"A sure thing. Joseph also said we're going to have three children together."

"Three!" she yelled, playing along with Joseph's *vision*. It felt nice to have hope, something innocent to cling to in the face of the threat before them. "I was thinking more like one."

"Hey, I'm just quoting the kid."

Blane walked over. "Play time is over. Do you want the command back?" he asked August.

He let Nikki drop to the ground. "No, you take it since I'm going to be on the front line."

"Be careful," Nikki whispered and hugged him tight.

"I'm Immortal, Nikki. They can't hurt me."

She thought of Tyras' arms with muscle like corded rope and the way he pinned August to the wall with the flick of a wrist. "Tyras might be able to."

"No, he can't. I took that beating in the cells for a reason. I wanted him to think me weak and not a threat so that he would leave us alone together. It was my only chance to get you out of there."

She nodded. It all made perfect sense, but it still didn't stop the worm of fear eating away at her insides.

Kade ran up to them. "Hurry, the soldiers have mobilized."

Together, they hurried back to the timber bunker. Across the distance that separated them, the soldiers of

Camp Drexton poured out of the training center and formed into battle lines.

August's mouth lifted in a savage grin. "It begins."

CHAPTER 18

Fiery Demands

Tyras steered the car to the side of the road and pushed the lever upward as far as it would go. The vehicle bucked to a hard stop as a result. He muttered a bloody curse and slammed out of the car, grateful to be free of the blasted contraption at last.

His impromptu driving lesson left a lot to be desired but in all fairness to his teacher, she had been ill at the time. Stella died on him somewhere in the middle of a piece of land she called Virginia, his close presence too much for her. Fortunately, a young man happened by to see if he needed assistance. He died an hour ago, but not before telling Tyras what to look for.

He glanced up at the large gate flanked by two pillars. Although, he could not read the writing on the sign, this was undoubtedly Camp Drexton. He could sense the presence of the Kjin on duty just beyond the gate.

Preferring anonymity until he found Billingsley, he pulled the collar of his coat up against the rain and skirted the main entrance. Instead, he plunged into the darkened woods that surrounded the camp on all sides. Within a few short yards, he detected a large gathering of Kjin to the west.

To the west it is then. I'm coming for you Nicola.

❧

The torrential downpour and deepening night hid the approaching army from sight, but August could hear them. The sounds that reached him were small. Soft footfalls. A cough here and there. Readjustment of weapons.

Unfortunately, Joseph disappeared again before anyone could tell the Immortal of the plan. August just hoped he was close enough to contribute.

"Ready?" Vincent asked. "It's just you and me."

"Yeah, let's do it. I'll go in deep. You stay out front and do what you can."

At Vincent's nod, August took his dagger in hand and together they walked out across the tarmac. All seemed implausibly quiet for the sheer number of people in the area.

Vincent stopped at midpoint, but August shifted and surged ahead, his shadowy form flying just above the ground. A few seconds more and the Drexton soldiers finally came into view. A vanguard of perhaps fifty wearing night vision goggles strapped to their heads, running in a low crouch. And, all Kjin, August realized with feral satisfaction.

He went to work efficiently, his body and dagger slithering in an out of the spaces between the men and their ribs. He killed twenty before the demons realized they were being attacked. Shouts of concern rang out into the air. The main army behind the advance unit stopped marching and bright illumination flooded the area—the desire for stealth clearly over.

All lights trained on Vincent as he stood alone in the center of the tarmac and spun his lasso in a blinding cone that appeared solid.

August turned away and penetrated deeper into the crowd of soldiers. By their whispered conversations, he learned that the terrorist rumor had been hotly debated and now most believed the Knights to be simple trespassers out for kicks. As far as they were concerned, their goal was simply to take the intruders into custody without anyone getting hurt. None appeared ready or willing to do actual battle with civilians.

Keep thinking that way.

August continued to listen in.

"What the hell is that guy doing?"

"Some freak light show. It's pretty cool."

"Someone should shoot him." This from a Kjin, of course.

"Yeah, right. The dude might be nuts, but we're not going to kill him for it."

August hoped they still felt that way after Vincent started slaughtering half their number.

He turned back. All on the tarmac stood fascinated by the Immortal. Startled yells rang out as Vincent sent the hallowed whip slicing through the air at blinding speed toward the assembled army. The first Kjin disappeared at its touch.

It took a few more kills for blind panic to set in and the army to realize it wasn't a freak light show after all. The smart humans—and cowardly Kjin—scattered for cover.

It's working. They're retreating.

August used the commotion to his advantage flowing through their ranks and ridding the world of the filth on his way to the training center. It was possible that Joseph had already taken Billingsley and Nash out, but August had to make sure.

He slid into the open door behind the streaming soldiers. Most of the bewildered mob congregated in the main hall and milled around awaiting orders. August moved to the back where the offices were located. The first two he glanced into were empty. At the third door, a pair of well-shod feet stuck out from under a table just inside. August glided in. He recognized the face from photos provided by Blane's team. Apparently, he wasn't the only one who wanted Governor Billingsley dead. The blood that still ran from the ragged slice across his throat told him it wasn't Joseph that killed him. Who then? Another Kjin? A human soldier? If it was a soldier, he or she would have unwittingly released the demon shade into the air and been transformed.

A loud scuffle came from the office next door. August flew out into the hall and hovered before the closed door. Shifting into physical form, he kicked the handle and sent the door slamming against the inside wall.

"Watch out!" The man who yelled the warning held a chair in his hands out in front of him to keep an attacking soldier at bay. August recognized the man as General Nash. One of the men he hunted.

In his fifties, he was of medium height, strong and athletic still, and with the unwavering eyes of a commander. He was dressed in casual clothes as though someone summoned him here from home. And, he wasn't Kjin. August couldn't say the same for his young assailant, though. Even if August's Kur hadn't told him the true nature of the kid, the twisting sneer would have.

August pulled his dagger from its sheath.

Nash narrowed his eyes at the weapon and jerked his chair back and forth between August and the demon.

With his eyes still on the General, August flipped his dagger to the side and with a soft thud, it embedded into the chest of the Kjin. The demon disappeared on contact and the dagger fell to the floor with an echoing clink.

"Shit!" Nash staggered back and swung his chair at August.

"Put the chair down," August told him. "I'm here to help."

"Not so sure I can take your word for that, pal," Nash said, licking his lips.

August walked over and retrieved his dagger from the floor. In a flash of movement he crossed over to Nash, ripped the chair from his hands and threw it to the ground. Before the General had time to react, August waved his dagger in his face.

The man's eyes glazed over for a moment before opening wide. His hand went to this head. "What's going on here?"

"What's going on is that the soldiers of Camp Drexton are in imminent danger. I want you to quickly evacuate...select...personnel."

"Select? Why?"

"Just do it. I'll send someone in to help you distinguish, and you can start funneling them out though the back of the facility."

Nash may have been a bureaucrat, but long-ingrained duty lifted his lip in a snarl. "You're talking about U.S. soldiers here. We fight. We don't run."

"You can't fight what's out there. Trust me. You'll only get innocent people killed if you try."

The General snorted. "Look, I have no idea who the hell you are, and too much has happened tonight for me to just take your word for it."

A figure darkened the open door. "Will you take mine?"

Sam Barnes stood in the entrance.

"Director Barnes," Nash greeted in astonishment and walked around the desk. "What are you doing here? Do you know what's going on?"

"I'll explain later. For now, we need to do as this man has just suggested and evacuate. I'll assist."

"The President?" August asked Sam.

"Safe. I thought you'd need all the help you could get here."

"I appreciate it. Make sure no one calls the authorities until this is done."

"Can't even if we wanted to," Nash chimed in. "Billingsley collected all cell phones and terminated communications access." He paused. "By the way, where is the Governor?"

"Dead."

Nash shrugged. "Can't say as I'm bothered by the news. The man wasn't stable, that's for sure. Hadn't been for a long time."

August nodded and left the men to their work. He shifted and bypassed the soldiers still assembled in small groups and went back outside. Sheets of rain fell from dark skies making it hard to see although he could detect a few lingering groups—mostly Kjin—gathered defiantly in front of Vincent.

The Immortal still waited in the middle of the tarmac. The Kjin had retreated enough that his lasso could no longer reach them, but he stood firm. A barrier to the Knights behind him. A rock in the river.

August lifted a hand to signal to him.

From out of nowhere, a fire ball the size of a boulder smashed into Vincent and sent him flying through the air. A gigantic figure in a knee-length, brush brown leather coat stalked into view. A relentless stream of fire flew from his fingertips, pinning the prone Immortal to the ground.

A wail of rage escaped August as he shifted and sprinted forward. He gagged at the smell of burning flesh and the Immortal's screams of agony. He tried to get closer to Vincent in an attempt to pull him free, but the heat of the otherworldly fire kept him back. For several hopeless moments, August could do nothing but watch in mute horror while Tyras destroyed his friend. When the devil finally cut off the torrent of fire, there was nothing left of Vincent except an unrecognizable, charred lump.

Tyras glared at the line of Knights along the bunker. "I am Tyras! You cannot defeat me! The more you resist, the more lives will be lost. Give me Nicola and you shall all walk free! I do not care about any of you. I do not fear you. You are meaningless. I only want Nicola!"

CHAPTER 19

Rampage

Every angelic eye turned toward Nikki, but hers were glued to Tyras. Terror raked at her insides making it impossible to breathe. Her legs started to buckle at the thought of being with him again. Still, she couldn't ignore the fact that she could end this now. All she had to do was make the ultimate sacrifice. One life for hundreds of others. What choice was there really? Even her fellow Knights would have to agree in the logic of such an exchange.

Yes, I have to go back to him.

On trembling legs, she took a step forward and felt massive movement all around her. The Knights of Emperica stepped in front of her, to the sides and behind, swallowing her in a wall of light, protecting her from evil.

Overwhelmed, Nikki staggered back and allowed herself something she never once did in Tyras' captivity. She wept. For the outpouring of love and solidarity, and for the undeniable bravery of her fellow Knights who never wavered a fraction in fulfilling their duty.

Could she say the same? For a brief second in time, she almost succumbed to the devil to selfishly end her own pain. Did she deserve such steadfast support? The fact that she couldn't answer with an unequivocal yes to those questions caused her to cry even harder.

"Very well!" She heard Tyras say. "Prepare yourselves for war."

◆

When the Knights closed his path to Nicola, Tyras fumed with anger, barely restraining the fire that hovered at his hands and ached to be unleashed.

"Hello, Tyras."

He twisted around in surprise. *Who would dare approach me this close?* Standing before him with an Emperical dagger clenched in his fist was the Knight who had taken his Nicola away from him. The Knight who invaded his lair and stolen his most precious treasure.

"You cannot have her," the Knight declared.

Tyras could not believe the gall of this young angel standing before him like a drowned rat with his blonde hair and what tried to serve as a beard plastered to his face. "Oh, but I will. On that you can be sure."

"She belongs to the light."

Tyras frowned at the choice of words.

"*Ego servo lucis!*" I serve the light.

Tyras hissed through his teeth at the indoctrinated phrase he remembered so well. "Who are you?"

The features on the face before him shifted until it morphed into the face of his ancient rival. He rocked back from the visage as though he'd been delivered a physical blow. "Antonius!"

"It is I, Tyras."

Tyras backed up another step and a red sword of fire sprang to life within his hand.

Antonius' mouth curled up in that infuriating smile Tyras remembered so well despite the passage of so many years. The dagger he held elongated into a sword of light. "Are you sure you want to do this, Tyras? I always was the better swordsman."

Tyras swiped his long hair off his brow and circled his enemy. "When we were peers, perhaps."

Antonius laughed. "Oh, you've elevated your station, have you? In the bowels of Mordeaux? I don't think so."

The time for games was over.

Tyras lunged. Antonius caught his blade and answered with a swift riposte that pierced him in the shoulder. Pain radiated up his arm, but he managed to keep his sword ablaze. He'd give it to Antonius. The Knight was as fast as ever. *I will have to be faster.*

Tyras attacked Antonius once again, their swords of fire and light clashing with the solidness of metal. Sparks pierced the gloom as they traded blows, and all the while, Antonius wore his contemptuous grin.

Tyras offered up a smirk of his own and summoned a ball of fire with his free hand, hurling it at Antonius.

The sword of light lifted in the air and swallowed the fire as though it had never been.

Damnation! Time to change tactics to the one recourse left when dealing with a better swordsman. Tyras roared and barreled forward, shoulder first. His powerful charge hit Antonius directly in the chest, sweeping his legs out from under him and sending him crashing to the soaked tarmac. The angel tried to stagger upright, but Tyras' foot was already moving in a brutal arc toward his face. Antonius' head whipped violently to the side from the force of the blow.

"August!" Nicola screamed.

Without thinking, Tyras swung his head toward the row of angels in disbelief. *Nicola cries for my enemy! How dare she?* Then, an errant thought hit him. *If Antonius is here...could it be possible?* He scanned the Knights until he found her, out in front, Aventi in hand. He took note of the familiar warrior stance. The way she held her sword with an index finger hooked over the crossguard. His gaze slid upward and as soon as their eyes met, he knew. *How did I not see it before?*

His mind in turmoil, he spun back around to the fight with Antonius, but his hesitation cost him. The Knight was already back on his feet and swinging. The sword of light hammered down directly across Tyras' wrist and severed his hand.

Tyras clutched his arm and bellowed in agony. Arterial blood spurted from the wound in a dark red spray. With his good hand, he created a wall of fire between him and his nemesis. Antonius sprang back, but several Knights—in a maddened desire to get to him—sprinted forward and tried to breach the wall.

A fatal mistake.

The elemental fire blazed hotter with malicious intent, scalding the bodies that made it through. Human infernos staggered in hopeless circles and wailed in misery. The flames of Mordeaux, impervious to the rain, showed no mercy. They sought, they consumed, they killed.

Tyras walk unsteadily from the battlefield and into the nearest building. "Tourniquet!"

A Kjin rushed forward and wrapped his arm at the elbow, but already the wound was healing over, creating a rounded hump of scar tissue where his hand used to be. His injury, however, didn't prevent him from noticing that there seemed to be far fewer soldiers than Governor Billingsley led him to believe would be here.

"Where's Billingsley?"

"Dead."

"Who is in charge here?" he demanded.

"No one, really."

"Is General Nash still contained?"

"I saw him head out the back with several soldiers."

The fire sword ignited in his good hand without thought and he started swinging in a murderous rampage. The shades of the two Kjin unfortunate enough to be standing closest to him exploded skyward when he beheaded their hosts. Another Kjin screamed and tried to run. A broad sweep of Tyras' sword amputated the demon's legs below the knees.

The others cowered back, creating a ring around him and the three corpses. The shades in the air hissed and zoomed around the ceiling before finally bursting into black ash.

Tyras froze. *There are no humans in the room.* "You idiots! Nash is taking the humans! Are there any left here?"

"There are close to a hundred locked in the back rooms."

"Find the rest! Take half of our number and retrieve those humans! We're at war, you bloody fools! We're going to need bodies!" He whipped around and lifted his fire sword above his head. "The rest of you set up in formation out front! It's time to kill angels!"

A guttural cheer reverberated throughout the hall.

Tyras pulled a gray-haired Kjin out of the circle by the scruff of his neck. "You're the new commander. If any angels are alive at the end of this night, you will spend eternity regretting it."

Chapter 20

Demons and Angels

A somber silence thicker than the wretched rain had been able to accomplish descended on the bunker. Nikki walked through the murky fog and found August standing alone, his jaw clenched tight as he studied the Kjin forming up across the tarmac. Or maybe he was looking at the burned heaps that had been relocated a short distance away. Six of the mounds lie unmoving, but the seventh twitched every now and then with a shallow, wheezing moan. The Immortal could not die. She wondered if he would eventually heal or be destined to remain on earth with a ruined husk of a body.

She placed a gentle hand on his arm. "August?" She paused. "Or should I call you Antonius?"

"I've been August Rand for many years," he answered without turning around. "You know me well enough. Or, should."

"Good, I'm kind of fond of August Rand."

"Fond?"

"Overly fond," she admitted.

"Now, those are words a man can fight for," he said softly but still had not looked at her.

"What are you thinking about?"

"That the last time we faced a battle like this, we both died."

"You keep making references to events I have no knowledge of." Yet, she believed him when he talked of them.

He finally turned to her and pulled her into his arms. "I know. I'm sorry. I just wish..."

"Wish what?" she prompted, eager to hear what tormented him so much.

But, he just shook his head. "Nothing. Just don't get yourself killed, okay? I lost you once and I really can't do it again."

"Did we love each other?" she asked, leaning back to look into his face.

At last. The smile she had been waiting for. "Very much."

"Show me."

He lifted a hand to stroke the side of her hair. His touch was gentle, but enough to ignite the same desire she felt for him in the car on the way here. Only more so because of the weight of love she now knew existed behind it.

Everything around her disappeared when their lips finally came together. The Kjin. The Knights. The rain. The fear.

His tongue swept inside her mouth, strong and demanding, as though this was the last kiss they would ever share. She refused to believe it. Yet, she moved her mouth against his with purpose. Committing to memory the taste and feel of his lips. Sensations that may have to last an eternity. His hands tunneled in her hair and dragged her face closer, something she didn't think possible. Circling his neck with her arms, she melted into him, body and soul, losing herself in his long, drugging kisses.

When he finally raised his head, she ached to pull him back. To spend just a few minutes more in the only safe haven she had ever known. "I wish I could remember," she whispered.

"Me, too," he said, but he didn't sound angry, just tired, like he had been dealing with her loss for a long time.

Again, she thought about ending this for him—for everyone. "It's me Tyras wants, August. Maybe I should just—"

"No."

"It could save lives."

"Maybe in the short term, but we still have to destroy him or else he'll take over the world. It might as well be here."

She simply nodded, not quite convinced. Tyras had made it clear in the way that he looked at her and the things that he said that she held some power over him. He desired her. Wanted her by his side. Shouldn't she take advantage of that power? "We're going to lose Knights."

"It's why we're here, isn't it? To fight demons."

"I suppose."

"Stop, Nikki. I know that look in your eyes. You're more valuable to us here. And, if Nash managed to get the humans out, we're not as outnumbered as before. We have a good chance." He let her go and pulled Vincent's lasso from his belt. "Think you can use this? It's the only weapon we have that might be able to keep Tyras' fire at bay."

She took it gingerly. "I'll do my best. No sign of Joseph yet? I'd feel better if there were another Immortal weapon out there."

August shook his head. "It's possible that he suffered the same fate as Vincent."

Nikki hoped not. An Immortal he may be, but he was still a child. The thought of him lying helpless and in pain sent a stab of anguish through her.

August held her shoulders. "It's time. Are you ready?"

She blew out a deep breath. "Yes."

"I love you, Nikki, just remember that. I always have and always will."

"I love you, too," she told him and meant it.

A wide smile lit up his face and it sent butterflies loose in her stomach. He took her hand, squeezed it, and together they walked back toward the line of waiting Knights. Instantly, Nikki felt their restlessness like a tangible hum in every shift of feet or exhaled breath. All they saw was the enemy in front of them.

Blane and Fallon silently fell in behind. Kade and Juliet were supposed to be in hiding in one of the empty buildings to the south, but knowing the two of them as well as she did, they were probably much closer, keeping an eye on their angel spouses.

Across the way, a gray-haired Kjin bellowed out the final order to his demons.

August stopped and faced the Knights. "There really isn't much for me to say!" he shouted so that as many as possible could hear his words. "But, there is a reason we were entrusted to lead this war against Tyras! Each one of us has the power and will to destroy this threat that stands before mankind. Let us be deserving of that trust today! Let us prove that the faith Emperica has shown in us is well placed!" He drew his dagger and lifted it over his head. Hundreds of angels did the same and the flare of their Aventis transformed night into day.

Nikki bounced on her heels, and shook out her hands—her warrior spirit demanding release. She watched the quivering tip of August's dagger with lip curled, nostrils flared, heart beating out of her chest. The adrenaline pounded through her veins, a righteous river that would not be denied.

With a defiant scream, August swung his dagger toward the enemy in a sweeping downward arc. The angels answered his call with shouts of their own and moved swiftly ahead, their line solid and unwavering. Hundreds of feet surged forward, the ominous thunder of their steps taking them inexorably closer to violence.

The Kjin answered the charge with one of their own.

Be safe, my love. Nikki peeled away from the group to find the space she needed to wield Vincent's lasso. And, not a moment too soon. She had to dive out of way as the two armies clashed with horrible impact. Vicious blades lashed out to slice angel skin. Aventis plunged into demon hearts, releasing shades into the air by the dozens.

"Nikki! Over here!"

She rolled to a stop and turned to the shout. Kade and Juliet hung out of a military jeep several yards away from the combat. She ran toward them.

"Thought you might need some height," Kade told her.

"I do," Nikki said and jumped up onto the hood of the jeep. She looked back at Blane's wife. "Didn't you promise your husband not to do this kind of thing?"

Juliet shrugged her slim shoulders. "I promised to stay away from the fighting. There's a lot of concrete and Kade Royce between me and the fighting."

Nikki shook her head at her friend. "Just stay at least thirty seconds away from those shades!" Planting her feet, she let the length of the whip out. She remembered seeing Vincent flick the tip toward the sky, so she mimicked his movements. When she was confident she had some control over the device, she snapped the tip of the lasso out into the mass of fighters. She felt the whip move of its own accord and strike out at one of the Kjin. When the demon vanished from sight, a grim smile of satisfaction lit up her face and she prepared for another throw.

Frightened shouts behind turned her around. A string of demons pursued the humans that had escaped out the back way. The fleeing soldiers branched off in all directions, hunkering down behind whatever vehicle or building they could find for cover.

Unfortunately, she wasn't the only one that heard the shouts. The demon shades over the battlefield swung en masse toward their location.

"Get down!" Nikki yelled at Kade and Juliet. She jumped on the roof of the jeep and swung her lasso at the oncoming horde. The tip sailed upward, but passed harmlessly through their mist. *It doesn't work on wraiths!*

The seething mass of grey swarmed over her head and toward the beleaguered humans.

"No!" she cried out helplessly. "There's no one to protect them!" *I can't watch this.* Young men and women destined to spend the rest of their lives trapped alongside a malevolent presence that would commit unconscionable sins with their bodies.

Juliet pointed. "Protection, incoming!" She hung out of the jeep window and waved her arms. "Hi, Penny!"

Nikki looked where Juliet waved. Her jaw fell open in shock at the white wall that swarmed forward to intercept the demon wraiths. Sentinels! Hundreds and hundreds of Sentinels! The Guardian Angels arrived to fight! Disbelief filled her as the normally placid angelic beings met the oncoming shades and tore into them with wild abandon.

"Go get 'em, Penny!" Juliet screamed.

Nikki had no time to figure out who Penny was. *There's still the Kjin to deal with.* She flew down off the jeep and flicked the lasso out ahead of her. The whip sliced toward the encroaching demons with unerring accuracy. She took half a dozen demons out as she ran. Drawing closer, she noticed with relief that there were a few Knights in the fray as well, helping the Sentinels.

She willed her feet faster and gritted her teeth in regret when one of the angels disappeared under the sharp machetes of a Kjin.

Arm muscles burning with pain, she continued to snap the whip with lightning speed. It finally worked. The Kjin in the rear of the pack broke from the danger posed by her Emperical weapon and retreated back toward the training center. That was all it took to scatter the remaining demons.

She waved at the humans. "Go! Go!"

Completely oblivious to the fight still raging in the skies above their heads, the soldiers took off.

A Knight in a dark suit and loose tie ran up to her. "Thanks for your help," he said wearily. "I'm Sam Barnes with the Secret Service."

"Oh, yes, August mentioned you."

He waved a hand back toward the escaping soldiers. "Don't worry, I'll round everyone up and make sure none remember what happened here today."

"Good. Just get them to safety. Are there any more humans inside?"

"Yes. There were still some in the back of the center that we couldn't get to."

"All right. We'll get them out."

"Good luck," he told her and took off, shouting to call the soldiers back together.

One problem solved. She gave a thankful salute to the Sentinels in the air and sprinted away. Kade and Juliet and their jeep were gone. *Another problem solved.* And, what she saw on the tarmac lifted her spirits even more. The Kjin seemed to once again be retreating and the Knights were making their way back to the bunker to regroup.

She started forward to join them, but then stopped.

The Kjin weren't leaving the battlefield as she thought. They were simply falling back to allow another group through to the front line.

Wait. What are they doing? She stepped closer, her steps halting as she tried to understand what she was seeing. *Dear, Lord.* Bile rose in her throat at sight of Tyras' new tactic.

Each Kjin in line had a human strapped to the front of their bodies.

Chapter 21

One of Our Own

The human shields wore many expressions. Some anger, others confusion. Most terror. The tandem forms ran forward and crashed into the retreating angels. Cries of surprise rang out as the Knights turned to fight only to halt their weapons mid-swing as they realized what they faced. The Kjin took advantage and carved into the angels, creating mortal wounds that for all their healing powers, they could not recover from.

The battlefield had turned into a murderous trap for the Knights. By the time the call for full retreat was sounded, it was too late for many. Several circles formed pitting the tandem fighters against the Knights in the center. With nowhere to go and powerless to fight back, the angels lost their lives.

Nikki searched frantically for August, but didn't see him. She did see Fallon stumble back from a furious slashing attack by one of the demons. The blonde Knight lost her balance and fell to the ground clutching her stomach in both hands. Not content to just kill, the demon bared a wolfish grin, lifted a heavy boot and stepped on Fallon's leg. Nikki heard the bone break even as Fallon's face contorted into a mask of pain.

Nikki's whip sailed toward the demon without conscious thought and caught the Kjin on the temple. Enough contact to blot him out of existence.

Fallon still twisted on the ground. Nikki raced to her. With no time to talk, she lifted her into the air and over her shoulder and sprinted back toward the bunker. Several angels were spread out on the ground under the wooden shelter out of the rain as they healed. Some would never heal.

Nikki wasn't surprised when Kade intercepted her to take his wife from her arms. Nikki gladly gave her up, anxious to find August and Blane. She turned to go and then stopped. "Hey, Kade."

The cop glanced over his shoulder.

"Congratulations."

A small smile lifted her lips at the look on his face, and she rushed back to the fight, the angels now in full retreat.

Her mind on Fallon's little miracle, it caught her completely off guard when she was hit from behind by a crushing blow. The lasso flew from her fingers. She watched in horror as her assailant scooped up the Emperical weapon and disappeared into the fighting mob.

Idiot! How could I be so careless? That weapon was all they had as protection against Tyras! With a growl, she flew to her feet and gave chase. She never slowed her steps as she crashed headlong into a chaotic nightmare where humans and angels screamed. The first in horror, the latter in pain. A river of red ran under her feet and it sickened her how much of it belonged to her angel warriors. Combatants who slipped, fell to their deaths on the blood-soaked tarmac.

With no time to mourn, she activated her Aventi and sliced a path through the demons without human captives. Up ahead, she caught glimpse of the Kjin with her lasso disappearing into the training center.

She slid to a stop. *Tyras is inside that center.* Although she considered it before, she had no desire to hand herself over to him. Not after August helped her see that it wouldn't stop the fighting, it would just take her out of it. She could do more for their cause on this side of the war instead of locked up somewhere as Tyras' plaything.

But, I still need that lasso! The Kjin and Tyras needed to be destroyed. Today. Why take a chance of them slipping away when they're right here on this battlefield?

Inevitably, a few of the cowards would escape, but if she could use the lasso to take out the majority, she could lessen the suffering by these creatures that murdered so indiscriminately. Fallon and Kade's unborn child could then inherit a world without demons in every corner. Blane and Juliet's little girls could be happy with their two new parents by their side. None of their lives would ever be perfect, but if she had anything to say about it, it could be free of Mordeaux's influence.

Mind made up, she pushed all fears to the side and sprinted toward the training center. Along the way, any Knight that needed another sword received it. Any demon that got within striking distance died.

Eventually, she fought her way clear to the door of the center. Stepping inside, she braced for a fight. But, it didn't come. The ground floor of the hall was empty.

"Nikki!" She glanced up to the open second level. A lone Knight waved his Aventi. "Be right down."

She waited impatiently, her eyes warily scanning the room. "Where are the Kjin?" she asked when the Knight made it down the stairs.

"Annihilated," he replied with a laugh.

"By who?"

"The little Immortal with the bow. He killed them all. Single-handedly."

Relief flooded through her that Joseph was still alive and in the fight. Could they be so lucky that he had also managed to take out the devil?

"Tyras?"

"Haven't seen him. But, hey, there's an Immortal weapon over there!"

Nikki followed the direction the Knight pointed. *The lasso!* She ran over to retrieve the weapon. The demon that stole it from her must have dropped it when he collided with one of Joseph's beams of light. *I will kiss that child when I see him next.*

She turned back to the Knight. "We better get back—"

An ominous whooshing sound cut off her words. Nikki threw her arms up against a sudden surge of heat that tore past her hot enough to singe her hair. The Knight wasn't so lucky. A fireball hit him square in the chest and swallowed him in flames.

Nikki ran and dove into the corner, just in time to avoid another fiery missile.

Tyras' evil laugh echoed around the room sending prickles of fear through her body. Scrambling behind a parked jeep, she sat with her back against the wheel and struggled to calm her beating heart. *I can't go back to him!* Nothing could frighten her more than what Tyras had the ability to do to her. Paralyze her. Break her. Use his lies to convince her to turn against the Creator. His torture and manipulation almost succeeded before August had shown up.

Another taunting laugh.

She scrambled to the other side of the jeep.

What does he want? If the fireballs were any indication, maybe he was more interested in killing her than in capturing her. She thought of Dr. Morris and Vincent and the Knights already fallen. She had to stop Tyras now even if it meant dying in the process. Anger replaced fear. Resolve flowed through her, strengthening heart, mind and soul. She stood and snapped out the whip. "Show yourself, devil!" she shouted and slowly made her way around the jeep.

Tyras stood leaning against the wall in an insolent pose. "Nicola. How lovely to see you again."

"You tried to kill me," she accused, moving closer to him.

"Actually, I didn't even realize it was you until the fire had already left my hands. Please accept my apologies. And, my bad aim."

"We end this now, Tyras. Just you and me."

"That's all I ever wanted." He held out a hand. "Come. I have a vehicle not too far away." A sudden thought wrinkled his forehead. "You can drive, can't you?"

She took another step. "No."

"You can't drive?"

"No, I'm not going anywhere with you. It ends here. Now."

She would have laughed at the confusion on his face if it wasn't so pathetic. He actually believed she wanted to be with him! How fitting that the master deceiver was just as adept at deceiving himself.

In a blur of movement, her hand shot out, the whip whistling toward Tyras' face. She knew it would take more than one strike to kill him, although how many she didn't know. She prepared to yank the whip back for another blow as soon as the first one fell, but it didn't get that far. The whip stopped inches from Tyras' face as though encased in cement. Tyras threw his hand out toward her, and the whip spun out of her hand.

"No!" She raced after weapon. In mid-sprint, she felt herself hoisted into the air by her throat. She kicked and clawed at her neck as Tyras pinned her a foot off the ground. Her lungs screamed for air. Panic seized her mind as blackness crept in at the edges of her vision.

"How could you do this to me?" Tyras wailed. "I love you, Nicola! I always have."

Tears ran down Nikki's face. Her head felt ready to explode. *Just let go. Home awaits.*

As convincing as her mind was, her body fought to stay alive. The will to live sent adrenaline pumping to her rapidly numbing limbs. *Let go. You wanted this.* Yes, but not before Tyras died.

"Why, Nicola? Why?"

Is he crying? Surely, the devil doesn't care for anyone but himself.

At last, her fingers fell from her throat and her arms dropped uselessly to her sides. Her eyes closed as she gave in to her persuasive thoughts and let go of the struggle to breathe. After all, air wasn't required where she was headed.

~⋽~

A small smile twitched on Nicola's lips one final time and then she went still. Horrified, Tyras released his hold and she fell to the floor in a crumpled heap. "What have I done?" he cried into the empty space. "Nicola!"

He backed away slowly as the realization hit him. She was dead. And, he killed her.

Why must I ruin all that I love? He snorted a mirthless laugh at that last word. *Only a few weeks returned and I've already allowed myself to think I can love? What a fool I have been!* His gaze snapped upward. *Oh, I see what you're trying to do. Your influence is strong here, but I will not fall into your trap! Love? I am the King of Chaos! I do not love! I bloody destroy!*

And, that's exactly what he intended to do. But, not here. He would not waste his time on this ridiculous petty fight. No, he had a bigger prize to win. The world!

With a last glance at the body on the ground, he lurched out through the back door and plunged into the woods behind the building. Blinded by grief and rage, he crashed forward. Trees groaned in protest at his passing, twisting into tortured dead skeletons at a single glance. Flowers and grass shriveled and died where he walked. Birds and animals tumbled dead from limbs.

This world mocks me!

Madness lurked at the edges of his mind. Despite the leafy canopy above his head, it now felt like there was too much space around him. Too much air. For the first time since arriving to earth, he longed for his underground dwelling.

I killed her.

The fire inside him roared to life and demanded to be released. Tyras obliged. Stumbling ahead, he threw fire as he went, burning all in his path. *I'll kill everything! I'll raze the world!* Soon, a gray thick smoke choked the path he walked. Large branches fell from trees. Twigs snapped and crackled. Wet leaves hissed as they burned. Everywhere, destruction! *Oh, how sweet the taste of revenge!*

A sudden, burning pain pierced through the soles of his boots and he looked down. Yellow flames licked over his feet and the bottom of his trousers. "Ah!" He stomped furiously to quench the blaze, but it wouldn't go out. Frantic attempts to bend the fire to his will failed. Dread took a hold of him as he realized the truth.

This world where life is treasured would not submit. Not the people or the fire or the damn flowers.

He ran then and didn't stop. This new insight that threatened his sanity propelled him forward in a wild charge. He ran until his legs threatened to give way beneath him. He outran the fire and the smoke and the battle. He outran it all.

Only when his strength failed, did he fall to the ground, exhausted.

No, I did not outrun it all.

He crawled until he could get back to his feet. Up ahead, a small cottage came into view. Rage now spent, he walked up the steps and went inside. There, in the middle of the floor on a threadbare carpet, he sank to his knees to wait.

It wouldn't be long now.

CHAPTER 22

Nikki's Truth

Soft tendrils of awareness pricked Nikki's subconscious. *Am I dreaming? Or, have I returned to Emperica?* Her mind worked to meld bits and pieces of memory together, but nothing fit. Every attempt just grew more distorted and unbelievable. So, she waited patiently, knowing the answers would come soon. A short time later, she felt a presence by her side.
Who's there? she dared ask even as she suspected.
It is I, my child.
Father?
Yes.
She felt both relief and disappointment. While she was happy to be back home, she also knew that the Creator depended on her in his eternal fight and if she was here with him, then she had failed.
Let me help you remember.

Remember what? she asked, but the answer soon came in the images that marched across her mind. Tyras. Her prison cell. Poati. Dr. Morris. The fighting. August. *Oh, August.* The fears he voiced during their night in the car together had been justified. Selfishly, she had convinced him to take a chance on her and now, as an Immortal, he alone would pay the price.

The Creator read her thoughts. *You are also Immortal.*

Me? How can that be?

You are one of the original twelve.

Her mind struggled to comprehend. *No. I've only just returned a few years ago, Father. Before that, I was the mortal daughter of Frank and Ava Falco.*

That is a memory you created for yourself.

Please, Father, I don't understand!

During the Holy War when the twelve was divided, Tyras tried to convince you to side with him and his three allies. However, your loyalty to me prevented you from following his plans.

So, I really am Nicola?

Yes.

Does Tyras know?

He suspects certainly. He saw the similarities and fell in love with you all over again.

Love?

Yes, he loved you then and still does. Despite all that he has become.

There were still too many missing pieces. *This is all so confusing. After I died with August, I went to Emperica and trained with Fallon, Blane and Julian. If I am an Immortal I wouldn't have gone through training with them.*

True, but there was a reason for it. If you will remember from your Knight studies, after I cast Tyras to Mordeaux at the end of the war, he made several attempts to escape. He was successful only once and unleashed the Kjin into the world at that time. The eight remaining angels—including you, Nicola—went back to earth to battle these demons. You have fought this fight for many, many years.

Then, why don't I remember?

In your last battle with Antonius as leader, the Kjin set an elaborate trap that cast you and the rest of the angels back to Emperica by way of a Ha'Basin. The process grievously wounded most of the angels and they "died" again as a result. Your memory was compromised and you had to start at the beginning and retrain as a Warrior Knight once again.

And, August?

August made it through unscathed, but he faced other battles since, namely his guilt at the failed mission and his unrequited love for you.

It was unrequited? she asked in surprise.

Yes.

Why?

Although you loved August very much, you put your duty above all else. That is precisely why he decided to remain in Emperica to train other Knights instead of returning to earth after the Ha'Basin incident. But, he never forgot you or all the years you spent fighting side by side. You are his true love and he is yours. Yet, you sacrificed that love and a family for duty. It is more than I should have asked.

It was all too much for her to comprehend. In time, she would try and digest all she had been told, but now all she cared about was returning to the fight. Returning to August. If she was Immortal, that meant she wasn't dead.

Again, the Creator read her thoughts. *You have given so much in my service, child. So many centuries you have fought. At long last, I owe you peace.*

No! I'm not ready, Father!

Find your peace, my child.

Nikki's body suddenly felt very heavy as though a great weight had been placed upon her chest. *No!* She sank rapidly, her mind screaming in protest. But, there was no turning back as she was pulled inexorably down...down...down.

∽∂∽

August slumped to the ground, fatigue spreading through his body. Thunder rumbled in from the west. Unrelenting, cold rain ran in his eyes and soaked him to the bone, but he didn't have the energy to wipe it away. After two brutal clashes against the demons, corpses littered the space between them. Remarkably, not a single one human. Most were angels, caught by surprise in the initial ambush. He finally succeeded in recalling the remaining Knights, but now the fate of the battle rested in his hands alone.

He had no choice—the Knights had to be sidelined. Their Aventis made shades. Given the closeness of the captives to their tormenters, one stab of an Aventi could send the demon wraith directly into the body of a human. There was just no getting around the tandem horrors except with an Immortal weapon.

And, he was all that was left.

It would be nice to have Joseph and his bow or Nikki and her lasso—preferably both—right now, but unfortunately, neither one of them could be found.

Where are they?

He could only guess that they were fighting their own fight inside the training center. It was the only explanation for their absence that he would allow himself to believe.

All night, August waited for the hundreds of Kjin in the center to come to the aid of their fellow demons, but they never came.

What are they waiting for? Why aren't they returning to the fight?

Wearily, he got to his feet when he saw the demons form into ranks again. The blood splattered human soldiers hung listlessly from their straps, numb to the carnage they witnessed.

August understood the feeling.

This is it. One last charge. It's all I have left to give. One way or another, the battle is about to be decided.

Blane appeared at his side, bruised and beaten. Fallon recuperated under the bunker with her husband. Alive, but healing a broken leg.

"Here they come," Blane hissed.

The sound of hundreds of boots pounding over the tarmac sounded thunderous in August's ears. "Blane, see what you can find out about what's going on inside the center. I'm worried about Nikki and Joseph."

Blane frowned as he watched the demons come. "You may need me here."

"I need Immortal weapons more. My dagger is not meant for long-distance strikes." He looked back toward the center. "Don't engage. Just find out what's going on."

"All right, I'll go now," Blane started away and then stopped and put a hand on August's shoulder. "You can do this, I know you can. But, forget about finesse. Keep your body low and stance wide. Shift frequently. You have the power to end this right now."

"I thought so, too, about two hours ago."

"Well, think it again, warrior." With that, Blane took off at a sprint, circumventing the army for the back entrance to the center.

August watched him go for a second longer and then put all thoughts out of his mind as he focused on the job ahead.

The sound of movement behind turned him around. The Knights were getting to their feet, some with assistance due to their injuries. They created two lines on either side of him, their Aventis raised in salute. For him.

"*Fari Creatoris!*"

"For August Rand!"

"You got this, August!"

August swallowed and finally wiped that damn rain out of his eyes. With a grateful nod, he ran through the tunnel of Knights and surged ahead alone to meet the oncoming horde. The shouts from the Knights followed him, filling him with their confidence.

The cowardly Kjin shifted ranks at his approach. With knowledge now of what he was capable of, they positioned the demons with human soldiers out front. Some of the humans didn't even look conscious—their heads flopping on bodies tied arms, legs and waist to their demon puppeteers. Others were very awake, and had come to learn in the long hours who the real enemy was. A few tried to fight back early on, but it had been a futile exercise with so many demons to menace them into compliance.

August ran harder, closing the distance.

Halfway, he shifted and flew over the heads of the human targets. He landed smoothly on the other side, returned to physical form and put his dagger to use—a deadly serpent striking impossibly fast and fatally accurate. Confusion dominated as demons in the rear of the pack started to die and those in the front realized their foe had vanished.

Some of the braver Kjin came at August when they saw him, their wicked looking knives slashing in at him from all directions. He caught each and every one. The demons didn't stand a chance. Not against Emperical light. All those he managed to touch disappeared in a flash of white.

A sharp jab to his back pitched him forward, and he knew he'd been stabbed. Although it wouldn't kill him, it hurt. Bad. He growled through the pain and swung his arm backward, sending the owner of the knife back to hell with a dagger through the gut. But, the movement sent him off balance and he lost his footing on the slick surface. Before he could recover, two demons slammed into him, taking him to the ground. He managed to slide away the thrusts meant for his throat, but others found their mark.

He shifted.

Reappearing at the left side of the group, he gritted his teeth and repeated the process. *It's taking too long.* With all his success, he would tire long before he destroyed all those without hostages. Somehow he had to finish this. Blane said he had the power to do it. But how? There was only one of him and a whole lot of demons. *I'm alone here.* Then, August remembered the Black Knights summoning lightning from Mordeaux. Could he call on Emperica for help? Would they even answer?

The certainty that they *would* hear his call almost took him to his knees.

I'm not alone. I never have been.

August shifted again and reappeared in the space between the two opposing forces. With the rain pouring down, he thrust his dagger into the air. The words came naturally. *"Ego servo lucis! Ego sum non unus!"* I serve the light! I am not alone!

All fell silent.

August stood with his weapon held high, in the dark and rain, and prayed for help. Prayed it would come before the demons decided to come at him. His arm quivered from fatigue and strain. *Please, I can't do this alone.*

Vile curses and shouts came from the demons as they goaded each other on. "Get him!" they hissed. "Slice him to pieces!" The taunts worked. With harsh, deafening yells, a group peeled away and rushed at him.

I need help!

And, it came.

A flash brighter than a thousand suns ripped from the sky in a crackling bolt of energy so immense every hair on August stood straight up from his body. He caught the beam of light on the tip of his dagger, terrified that he would be crushed under the weight of such absolute power. But, it didn't crush him. Instead, the essence filled him and made him stronger. His vision sharpened in the gloom. His hearing improved. New life poured into his muscles, erasing the tiredness from his mind and body.

The Knights' war cries rang out into the night shattering the silence and urging August to use the gift that he had been granted.

Grunting with effort, he jerked his dagger toward the host of demons and lightning shot from the weapon. The deadly light tore through the evil horde, skipping through their ranks and eradicating every Kjin it touched. August couldn't stand by while the light did its work. He tore after those that thought to escape and struck at them in fast measured blows. Demon after demon disappeared from sight. Half-mad with the Emperical power that infused him from the dagger, he killed with a vengeance.

No Kjin blade touched him again.

He was invincible.

When he was done, all that was left on the tarmac were a hundred confused humans. Some collapsed to the ground and others standing in terrified disbelief at the vanished army.

Blood soaked August's clothes. Satisfaction lifted his lips in a snarl. He fell to his knees with his fists outstretched overhead. "I won, Tyras! We won! Your army is defeated! Come out and face me now!"

A ragged laugh tore from his throat. *It's over. It's finally over.*

"August!"

He lurched to his feet, drunk on victory and power. Through the rain, a lone man approached. Blane walked toward him carrying a limp figure in his arms.

August swept his wet hair back on his head and moved closer.

"No," he moaned.

It looked like a child in Blane's arms, but he knew it wasn't. His joy turned to agony. A second ago he had a future filled with hope and now he had nothing.

When Blane stopped in front of him, he reached out and tenderly stroked Nikki's cheek. It felt cold to the touch.

He had tried to harden his heart against this possibility, but Nikki wouldn't have any of it and tore through all his barriers, leaving him exposed. In that moment, though, his thoughts weren't on the pain—there would a lifetime to deal with that. No, his only wish was that she had remembered their life together. Their real life, not the false memory. If she had, it would have been easier to move on. Because without her validation, his own life had been nothing but a lie.

"We were almost there, baby," he chastised her gently. "We were almost there." He leaned down and pressed his cheek to hers. "I know I told you that if I couldn't spend a lifetime with you, it wouldn't be enough, but I was wrong. I loved every minute we had and if I could have just a second more, I'd take it."

He straightened and looked at Blane. "Give her to me." Blane carefully transferred her to his arms. "Round up the humans and erase their memories," he ordered.

With his precious bundle tight in his arms, he walked off the field of battle.

CHAPTER 23

Balance

Tyras waited and listened. The only sounds in the air the pattering of rain outside and the creak of the rocking chair beneath him. Patience had certainly never been one of his virtues, but he thought it downright rude to keep him waiting this long.

Through the open door, the smell of wet, burnt wood drifted to him. Ah, it would seem the fire had also lost its bid for dominance here.

He pulled his coat tight around him and shivered. *Why is it so cold here? Seventy degrees is simply uncivilized.* He threw his hand out and let loose a small spark of fire toward the rustic fireplace next to him. The wood flared to life and the dancing flames cast hypnotic shadows along the hearth. His attention on his newly created blaze, he almost missed the light that lit up the darkened woods beyond his small refuge.

About time.

The halo of light moved closer, too bright to identify the figure at the center of it, yet, of course, he knew. Silently the nimbus came on. Quite an unremarkable approach really for all that the light represented.

Suddenly, the radiant ball that was yards away, zipped directly into the small cottage, blotting out all sight and thought. Startled, Tyras shielded his eyes and fell from his chair. Blinding pain stabbed into his temples.

"YOU HAVE PROVOKED ME UNTO WRATH FOR THE LAST TIME, DRAGON!"

Tyras trembled before his maker, incapable of speech.

"HOW DARE YOU SLITHER OUT OF YOUR EXILE FOR THE PURPOSE OF DESTROYING WHAT I CREATED?"

Tyras shrieked in agony and writhed on the ground, his boots pounding helplessly into the wooden floor beneath him.

"YOUR REBELLION IS OVER, TYRAS!"

At this last declaration, the cottage exploded apart. The walls and ceiling disappeared in a violent maelstrom of wood and stone. Tyras covered his head as broken pieces of the structure and furniture rained down and thudded into his body. A roiling black cloud spun into existence above him. Earsplitting thunder boomed inches from his head. Bolts of lightning struck down all around threatening to electrocute him with every sizzling crack.

"Please stop, Father. I...I apologize. I know it sounds ridiculous coming from me, but it's the truth."

The Creator could not possibly have heard him as he spoke barely above a whisper, but the second he said the words, the storm stopped. Not only the storm, but the rain that had harassed his every step since he arrived.

Cautiously, Tyras lifted his head from underneath his arms. He sucked in a breath in awe. Golden rays of the rising sun peeked through the trees on the eastern horizon, and he couldn't tear his eyes from the sight.

A polite cough brought him back and he pushed himself into a sitting position on the wooden floor, all that was left of the cottage.

Before him stood a young boy.

Tyras rubbed his thick jaw. "Interesting. Yes, indeed. Is there a point here, Father?"

"Perhaps."

"You spared my life."

"Yes."

"Why? I don't belong here."

"No, you do not."

He issued a grim laugh. "You really messed up with me, Father, didn't you?"

"Do not seek to place blame. You were given free will and you made your own choices."

"But, I was filled with hate, almost from the very beginning. I coveted. I murdered. I thieved. There was no compromise in me. Ever. Why?"

"Envy and greed took root in you early on. Without the proper balance to temper your choices, you went astray. It is the reason I created earth."

"Balance?"

"In the face of temptation, faith, love and charity must be embraced. Without these virtues, one simply cannot appreciate all that is Emperica. You are proof of that."

Tyras snorted. "My faith and charity were clearly lacking, Father, I agree. But, I did love. Not only Nicola. I loved you very much at one time."

"I know."

"I may never find this balance you speak of."

"No, but your heart is not as black as it once was." With a hand gesture by the Creator, a gateway to Mordeaux sprang open in the air. "It is time."

Spitting, red scaled demons screeched and threw themselves at the portal when they saw it appear, but they were unable to breach the one-way access point.

Tyras stood and pulled the ragged, dirty lace of his shirt through his sleeves. He turned to go, but paused to look back wondering if he would ever see his maker again.

The Creator did not smile, but Tyras detected a note of forgiveness in his voice when he said, "We will meet again."

Tyras nodded once and slipped through the portal.

⁓⑤

Carefully, August laid Nikki down on a coat someone draped on the ground beneath the tarp. Knights converged around him, but August just wanted them gone. Every one of them. Their consoling touches and whispered words. It was too much. Too invasive.

He was about to tell them so when a huge explosion sounded from the forest at the back of the training center.

"What was that?" someone asked.

"August, should we investigate?" another inquired tentatively. "If you'd rather we stay with—"

"Go! Just go! All of you." He couldn't care less about the explosion. He just wanted to be alone with Nikki one last time.

He heard them leave and knelt beside her. His fingers brushed back the hair from her face. One could easily believe her sleeping if not for the pale bluish tint to her skin. She still looked perfect to him. The strength and spirit packed into this one little body never failed to move him.

He checked her for wounds, but found nothing, making him wonder how she had died. By Tyras' own hand? With grief heavy on his mind, he never thought to ask Blane what had become of the devil.

He leaned down and placed his lips on hers. "I'm kind of mad at you for leaving me behind like this, you know. I really needed you here to watch my back. Who's going to tease me and make me laugh? Definitely, not Blane," he admitted with a tortured laugh. His thumb rubbed her cheek. "You're the only one who ever made me feel...human. Kind of funny coming from an Immortal, huh?" He sniffed. "Well, I guess this is it, baby. You're safe and happy now. That's all that really matters."

A soft shuffling behind him caught his attention and he scrubbed his eyes before turning around.

Not everyone had left after all. Blane, Juliet, Fallon and Kade remained. He wanted to be angry at them for witnessing this private moment, but he realized they loved her just as much as he did. Although, his face did color slightly at realizing Blane heard his joke about him.

"It stopped raining," Juliet said softly into the silence.

Such a trifling observation, but after weeks of sloshing through the stuff, it probably held significance that should be important to him. It wasn't. Not without Nikki. Never before had the yoke of duty pulled so tight around his neck. It felt lodged right in the middle of his throat and threatened to cut off his air supply with every swallow.

"Hey, look!"

He got to his feet at Fallon's shout. The Immortal, Joseph, walked across the tarmac, the rising sun at his back creating a halo effect behind him. August pushed through the others to meet him.

"You lied, Joseph!" he screamed, pointing an accusatory finger at him. "You said Nikki and I had a future together!"

Blane's rough grip stopped him from advancing. "Stop, August, it isn't the boy's fault."

"He lied!" August said again and shrugged Blane off him and walked away. "He lied and I believed him."

"She is Immortal, Antonius."

August stopped and swept his gaze back to Joseph. "I thought her immortality had been stripped from her?"

"No."

"Then, why is she not responding?" he demanded, hope filling him as he sprinted back to the tarp to see if what Joseph said could really be true. At Nikki's side, he dropped down to his knees and patted her cheeks. "Come on, baby, wake up. Wake up!"

"She does not wake due to Tyras' paralyzing touch. She needs my help." Joseph squatted and put a hand on Nikki's head. August was taken aback when the Immortal laid a hand on his head as well. He started to protest until a gentle, radiant energy surged inside him.

"What...?"

"My child, you and Nicola have sacrificed so much. Your immortality is no more. Go forth and live and love. Find your peace in each other."

My child? August fell back. "Father? Is it you?"

"Be at peace, Antonius. Tyras is sealed back in Mordeaux. Continue the fight." The blue eyes twinkled. "We are winning."

And, with that, he walked over to the charred remains of Vincent, placed a hand on his body and they were both gone.

Epilogue

Peace

Nikki's eyes fluttered open and she felt the warm sun beating down on her face, something she hadn't enjoyed in a long time. But, if she was in Emperica, why did her head hurt so much? August's face swam into view above her. "Hi, baby. How are you feeling?" His voice sounded hoarse, like he'd been crying.
"Fine, I guess. Where am I?"
"Still here with me."
Happiness flooded into her. "Is the battle over?"
"Yes."
"Tyras?"
"Gone."
Her heart started pounding at the proximity of August. "Wait. I feel different."
"You are. You're no longer Immortal."

Her cheeks flushed. "Suddenly, all I want to do is kiss you."

"Do it."

⁂

Blane hit his forehead with his palm. "I called him the peanut gallery. The Creator!"

Juliet shrugged. "Well, I swore in front of him." She tilted her head. "Think I can still get into heaven?"

⁂

Kade rubbed Fallon's stomach. "A boy, huh?"

"Yes."

"I feel like the luckiest man alive."

"We've come a long way since that first kiss on my stoop in Alden."

"You had no chance. I'm special, remember?"

"You're right."

⁂

And, across television sets across the nation.

"Good evening, I'm Tamara Elliott, reporting to you live from Harris Center in New York. Once again, Camp Drexton is in the news with reports of an attack. There are several accounts about what happened on that military post in the middle of nowhere. Some fanatical. Some inspirational. Still awaiting official word, but some fear we may never know for sure." The blonde anchor turned her smile to a different camera. "The bigger news today is that the rain has finally stopped, America! How often is it that we don't appreciate the sun until it starts to rain? That we don't seek the light until we're plunged into darkness? Well, I don't know about you, folks, but there seems to be more at work here than Mother Nature. What do you think?"

The End

Afterword

This ends the Angels of the Knights trilogy. I can't thank you enough for taking the journey with Fallon, Kade, Blane, Juliet, Nikki and August.

It is an extremely sad moment for me having to give them up now, but I know they're happy and in good hands.

Onward to the next adventure!

My best to you all.

Valerie Zambito
www.valeriezambito.com

About The Author

Valerie Zambito lives in New York with her family. A great love of world building, character creation, and all things magic led to the publication of her epic fantasy series, ISLAND SHIFTERS, in October, 2011. The first book in her paranormal fantasy series, ANGELS OF THE KNIGHTS, followed the following year in 2012. Visit www.valeriezambito.com for the latest information.

Books Published by Valerie Zambito:

Book One: Island Shifters - An Oath of the Blood
Book Two: Island Shifters - An Oath of the Mage
Book Three: Island Shifters - An Oath of the Children
Book Four: Island Shifters - An Oath of the Kings
Angels of the Knights - Fallon
Angels of the Knights - Blane
Angels of the Knights - Nikki

Printed in Great Britain
by Amazon.co.uk, Ltd.,
Marston Gate.